P9-BAW-465

TIME'S MEMORY

TIME'S MEMORY

JULIUS LESTER

COCHRAN PUBLIC LIBRARY
174 BURKE STREET
STOCKBRIDGE, GA 30281

FARRAR STRAUS GIROUX · NEW YORK

HENRY COUNTY LIBRARY SYSTEM
HAMPTON, LOCUST GROVE, McDONOUGH, STOCKBRIDGE

Copyright © 2006 by Julius Lester
All rights reserved
Distributed in Canada by Douglas & McIntyre Ltd.
Printed in the United States of America
Designed by Barbara Grzeslo
First edition, 2006
1   3   5   7   9   10   8   6   4   2

www.fsgkidsbooks.com

Library of Congress Cataloging-in-Publication Data
Lester, Julius.
    Time's memory / Julius Lester.— 1st ed.
       p.   cm.
    Summary: Ekundayo, a Dogon spirit brought to America from Africa,
inhabits the body of a young African American slave on a Virginia
plantation, where he experiences loss, sorrow, and reconciliation in the
months preceding the Civil War.
    ISBN-13: 978-0-374-37178-4
    ISBN-10: 0-374-37178-4
    [1. African Americans—History—19th century—Juvenile fiction.
2. African Americans—History—19th century—Fiction.   3. Dogon
(African people)—Religion—Fiction.   4. Space and time—Fiction.
5. Slavery—Fiction.   6. Plantation life—Virginia—Fiction.
7. Virginia—History—1775–1865—Fiction.]   I. Title.

PZ7.L5629 Tim 2006
[Fic]—dc22
                                                                    2005047716

In memory of Anne Romaine

TIME'S MEMORY

PROLOGUE

Our lives do not begin when we are born. Only our bodies do. Our lives begin so long ago that only Time remembers when and where and, most important, why. Our lives begin in a past of which we have no knowledge. They extend into a future we cannot imagine.

We are more than our personal memories. There are the memories our parents and grandparents share with us about their lives and the lives of their parents. Those memories help shape us and mold our lives into forms they could not have otherwise. But what about the lives and memories of those our parents and grandparents do not remember and know nothing of? What about those of our ancestors whose names we do not even know? Could it be that we are also shaped by memories no one remembers?

A hundred years from now, no one will remember that you and I ever existed. Nothing will remain except our names on tombstones, maybe. But we will not be dead, only not remembered.

My great-grandfather came from the plains of western Africa, where land and sky are flat and the horizon is farther away than the eye can penetrate. His name was Ekundayo, and he was sent to this land by Amma, the creator god of his people and the master of life and death. I am the last of his descendants, the one he chose to tell his story—and mine. It is a story I hope you listen to and hear in the very depths of your being. Whether humanity has a future may depend on it.

Nathaniel Ekundayo

PART ONE

1

T his is my last trip," Josiah Willingham muttered to himself.

It had been a week since the slave ship sailed from Guinea with its black cargo. For a week the screams, moans, and cries of the blacks in the hold had not stopped.

"Can't do it no more and I won't." He refilled his glass with rum, closed his eyes, and drank it down in two quick swallows.

Josiah was a tall, thin man with a sharp nose and small lips. His black hair was parted in the middle and brushed tightly down on both sides of his head. Despite the severity of his features, there was a gentleness about him which showed in the sad softness of his dark eyes. He looked like he should have been in the pulpit of some small country church telling his congregants about God's love. But a loving God, he felt, would not have taken his Hannah, who died after giving birth to their daughter, who lived but a few hours longer than her mother.

That was when he lost his way. After burying his wife and daughter, he left the tiny island off the South Carolina coast where he and Hannah had dreamed and loved. He had no idea where to go or what to do, and he had not cared.

One day, he found himself walking near the docks in Charleston. A man stopped him and asked if he wanted to go to sea. Josiah said yes. Surely, he thought, he would stop grieving for Hannah when he was surrounded by nothing but water. Even if he had known he was hiring on to a slave ship, it saddened him to think he probably would have gone anyway. But four years ago, he hadn't cared about anything or anyone, especially himself.

On the voyage out, being at sea was what he needed. He found himself smiling at the sight of whales swimming just beneath the surface and porpoises leaping out of the water, sailing through the air and back into the water to swim alongside the ship with astonishing speed.

Eventually the ship reached its destination, the west coast of Africa. Until that day, Josiah had never thought about where slaves came from. They were as much a part of the South Carolina landscape as the moss that hung from tree limbs. He had been too poor to own slaves, but if he'd had the money, he would have wanted one or two to help with the work. But he knew Hannah would have made him choose between her and slaves, and that was no choice.

On that first voyage, Josiah's job had been to take the blacks down into the darkness of the ship's hold as they were brought on board. He forced them onto their sides, with knees drawn up, to lie next to each other like spoons in a drawer. He had tried to be indifferent and unfeeling like the other white men on the ship. But the blacks looked at him with desperation in their tear-filled eyes, crying and screaming. He did not understand a word they said, but he didn't need an interpreter to tell him they were pleading to have their lives returned to them. To his ears their cries sounded no different than the ones he had wailed aloud in the hard solitude of his little cabin on the island, cries that still keened but were audible to his ears alone.

Once the ship set sail for Charleston, he went into the hold each morning and brought the slaves on deck to be exercised. While two crew members played a drum and flute, the others forced the slaves to dance. Josiah, however, went back down into the stifling heat and unbearable smells of sweat, fear, excrement, and urine. Invariably, there was a body or two he had to put on his shoulder, bring topside, and toss into the ocean.

That was how he learned that sharks swam behind slave ships, waiting for the inevitable bodies. He vomited the first time he saw sharks thrashing the water as their mouths of sharp teeth tore into the black flesh and turned the blue water a dark red. The other crew members laughed, at both him and the screaming blacks. He never threw up again, but only because he closed his eyes as he pitched the bodies overboard and tried not to listen to the sound of the churning, roiling water.

After the bodies were disposed of, he went below again with buckets of water and a mop and cleaned the hold of the slaves' waste matter. Even though he hadn't been assigned to that job since the second voyage, he thought he would smell the stench for the rest of his life. But he'd only had to smell it. The blacks had to lie in it. He still didn't understand how, at voyage's end, any of them emerged alive. But they did, and then walked down the plank and onto the dock to begin their lives anew in a place whose existence they had not known of, with people who did not look like them or speak a language any of them knew. If he had been black, he doubted that he would have survived the voyage. And if by some stroke of misfortune he had, he could not imagine living, day in and day out, year in and year out, as another man's property to do with as he saw fit.

When that first voyage ended and the ship docked at Charleston, Josiah swore he would never hire out on another slaver. But eventually the money he'd earned ran out, and he hired on to another ship, not knowing what else to do.

Elijah Wright had been the captain of that second ship. Josiah hoped he would never again encounter a man so evil. He had treated the crew only a little better than the slaves, and if anyone complained, Elijah had him tied to the mainsail to be buffeted by the winds until the man's screams and sobs became unbearable.

If Josiah had been distressed by how the slaves had been packed in the hold on his first voyage, his distress turned to anger when Elijah put so many slaves in the hold that the ship rode lower in the water than was safe. But Elijah Wright's theory was that many were going to die anyway. The more niggers he could squeeze into the hold, the better chance he had of arriving in Charleston with a profitable load.

So many slaves were dead when Josiah went into the hold each morning that other crew members had to help him carry the bodies up and throw them overboard. However, those who were sick, perhaps near death even, were to be pitied more than the dead. Elijah Wright did not make distinctions between the dead and near dead. Josiah didn't like remembering the blacks he'd pitched overboard, eyes wide in horror, screams of terror tearing their throats as they realized what was happening to them. So many were thrown overboard on that voyage even the sharks became sated and left bodies to float like seaweed before sinking slowly into the black depths.

Perhaps it was the combination of the crew having to eat too much salt pork and hard crackers, Elijah's evil temper, and the screams and stench from the hold permeating the entire ship. Whatever it was, Josiah was not the only one who, midway through the voyage back, had had more than enough. One morning, he led the men to Elijah's cabin, grabbed the captain, and pitched him overboard, as oblivious to his screams as the captain had been to those of the slaves. Josiah was at the helm when the ship returned to Charleston. He explained to the ship's owners that Elijah Wright had been washed overboard during a storm. They cared less about Elijah's fate than that Josiah had brought back a full load of slaves. They made him captain of the next ship they sent out.

Josiah was determined to be a better slave ship captain than the two men he had served under. Instead of packing the slaves in the hold like spoons, he took on fewer and laid them on their backs with space between them. While fewer died from disease, many more died than he'd expected.

Josiah didn't know how they did it. They seemed to make up their minds that they didn't want to live, and almost overnight they were dead. What kind of power of mind did these blacks have that they could commit suicide by thought?

When Josiah reached Charleston with little more than half the number of blacks he had left Africa with, he knew the ship's owners would barely make a profit when they put the slaves up for auction. They financed one more voyage under his command, with the understanding that this would be his last if he didn't bring back a sufficient number of slaves.

But Josiah could not bring himself to fill the hold as he knew he should. Sometimes he felt that Hannah was looking over his shoulder, approving or disapproving of everything he did, and she didn't like him being on slave ships. Pleasing her, dead though she was, was more important to him than pleasing the men who paid him. He knew his days on a slave ship were over after this voyage.

Just as he refilled his glass with rum, a loud shriek came up from below and through the floor of his cabin. Josiah put his hands over his ears, but other voices joined the shrieking one. It seemed as if the hold was filled not with people but with the cries wounds would make if they had voices.

The door to his cabin swung open. "Captain Willingham? Aren't you going to do something about that god-awful racket?"

Josiah looked at Wallace Troy, the man he had chosen as his second-in-command because of his years of experience on ships of all kind. Josiah was sorry he had not known that Troy had as few morals as Elijah Wright. "And what do you propose I do about that god-awful racket, Mr. Troy?"

Troy looked at the bottle of rum sitting in the center of the table and how tightly Willingham was holding his half-full glass. Wallace Troy didn't bother to hide his contempt for the captain as a sneer spread across his face.

"When I was second-in-command to Captain Rodney Miller, he went into the hold with his rifle, put the barrel down the throat of one of them, and pulled the trigger. We didn't hear a sound for the rest of the voyage."

Josiah looked at Wallace with as much contempt as Wallace directed at him. "I've heard of Rodney Miller. The man is unfit for human company. There'll be none of Rodney Miller's cruel methods on my ship. Is that clear, Mr. Troy?"

"That screaming is about to drive the men crazy!"

"Let me ask you something, Mr. Troy."

"What's that?"

"Would you scream if you had just been stolen from your homeland, cuffed and shackled, put into the hold of a ship that was going to take you to a place you never knew existed, and, once you arrived, you found out you were going to work the rest of your life for nothing? Would you scream, Mr. Troy?"

That was why Wallace Troy hated Josiah Willingham. He talked like a Yankee abolitionist and not like a white man was supposed to. Every right-thinking white man knew niggers didn't have feelings like white people. That black skin of theirs made them less sensitive and less aware of what was going on. Slavery was a blessing because it brought niggers into contact with whites. Just being around white people would civilize them, as much as that was possible.

"Would you scream, Mr. Troy?" Josiah repeated the question, louder.

"If something's not done about that noise, you might find yourself on the other end of a mutiny like the one I heard you led."

"And would this one be led by you, Mr. Troy?"

Wallace Troy turned around abruptly and walked out of the cabin, slamming the door behind him.

Josiah raised the glass to his mouth, then stopped and set it down. He had to keep his wits about him. Troy was dangerous. Even if Josiah found a way to quiet the blacks, that didn't guarantee he would make it back safely to Charleston. But if he didn't get them to stop their infernal screaming, there was no doubt the crew would throw him overboard like garbage.

As Josiah started to get up, the ship suddenly began rocking violently from side to side. He stumbled and almost fell before managing to regain his balance. Outside, the wind was howling and rain slapped hard onto the deck and the roof of his cabin. A storm had come up, but from where? When he had come to his cabin a short while ago, the sky was clear in every direction.

In the hold the screaming grew in intensity and strength until it was almost as loud as the wind and the rain. The ship was pitching violently now. The bottle and glass of rum fell off the table, the glass shattering as it hit the floor. Josiah tried to get to the door, but it was like walking up a steep hill. He was reaching for the knob when the ship rolled sharply to the other side. Josiah and the shards of glass on the floor were hurled in the opposite direction.

"Captain! Captain!" Josiah heard Wallace Troy's voice from outside. Willingham wasn't sure, but he thought he heard fear in Troy's voice.

Josiah finally reached the door and stumbled onto the deck. He raised his forearm against the hard-driving rain that immediately soaked him, stinging his flesh like swarms of bees. Huge waves crashed over the bow of the ship, sending more water across the deck and drenching the men who were roping themselves together and tying the rope to the mainmast to keep from being swept overboard.

"This storm came out of nowhere!" Troy yelled in the captain's ear. "From nowhere! One minute it was bright and sunny and the sea was calm. In less time than it took me to blink my eyes, the blackest clouds I've ever seen rolled across the sky and the winds came up. It's the niggers! I know it is! That screaming they're doing, that's what brought this storm. They're devils and heathens. The men are ready to go down below and pitch them all overboard. It's the only way to save ourselves! You hear me? It's the only way!"

"I'll take care of it!" Josiah shouted back.

"You better, or we will!"

Josiah staggered across the deck to the door to the ship's hold. It was all he could do to maintain his balance against the ship's rolling and the relentless rain. He finally managed to wrench the door open and step inside.

He stood there on the top step, holding tightly to the handrail that bordered the steps. The shrieking of the blacks was louder here, the sound assaulting him like hard fists.

What was he going to do? How was he going to make them stop? Josiah wasn't a superstitious man, but he was convinced that blacks had powers white men knew nothing of. He had no doubt they had called up this unnatural storm. But if they didn't put a stop to it, they were going to kill everyone, including themselves. Maybe that was what they wanted.

When his eyes adjusted to the darkness, he moved slowly down the stairs, clutching the handrail as the ship continued rolling. When he reached the last step it was as if someone or something pushed him. Josiah stumbled and had to reach out for the edge of one of the tiered bunks to keep from falling. Just as he did, the ship tilted violently. Josiah started slipping to the floor when hands came out of the blackness and grabbed his shirt. Josiah tried to pull away, but the screaming became louder and the very sound seemed to intensify the hold of the unseen hands.

This can't be happening! Josiah told himself as he continued struggling unsuccessfully to free himself. Then, amid all the screaming, he thought he heard something different. He stopped struggling and listened. Yes. There it was again! It couldn't be. But it was! A baby was crying! But he had looked over every one of the women before they were brought onto the ship and there had not been a pregnant one among them. At least not one so close to term that she would have given birth on the ship.

The child is still but a seed.

Josiah looked around, though he could see little in the blackness.

"Who said that?" he shouted back at the voice that sounded so familiar, so achingly familiar. "Hannah? Is that you? Hannah?"

Had he heard her actual voice, or just the one with which he conversed every day in his head?

It is me, Josiah.

Hannah! Oh, Hannah!

There is no time now, Josiah. They asked me to speak with you. What has become of you, Josiah Willingham?

Josiah didn't understand. How could he be having a conversation with Hannah? How could she hear what he was thinking, since he had not spoken aloud since calling out her name? Was he losing his mind?

Oh, Hannah! I have become a weak man since you left me.

Not so weak. You stood up to Wallace Troy, who wants to kill someone because he is afraid.

I won't be able to stop him if this storm doesn't stop.

You must do what they ask.

What? What do they want?

When the ship reaches Charleston, you will take every-
one out of this hold except one who will be hiding in the
shadows. When it is safe, you will take her away with you
and hide her where no one can find her, her and the child she
is carrying. If you promise to do this, the ship can resume its
voyage under blue skies and on a calm sea.

Josiah recognized that there came a moment in every
life when God asked one to choose good or evil. Was this
that moment in his? He felt incapable of responding, and
yet he knew he must or betray whatever little good remained in his soul, that good he knew as Hannah.

What is your answer, Josiah?

I will do it.

The shrieking cries ceased so quickly that the sudden
and unexpected silence was almost as hurtful to Josiah's
ears as the screaming had been. Whatever or whoever had
been holding him let go as the ship resumed sailing as
smoothly as if it were a canoe being rowed across a tran-
quil lake.

"Hannah?" Josiah called aloud.

There was no answer.

Hannah? he cried from within.

There was only silence. He stood for a moment, staring
fearfully at the tiered bunks where the blacks appeared to
be sleeping.

Who are you? he asked silently. *What are we doing*
bringing you across the ocean? What are we doing?

No one answered. Josiah trudged slowly up the stairs
and onto the deck. The glare of the sun in the clear blue
sky reflected off the still ocean with such brightness that

he flung his forearm before his eyes. When his eyes became accustomed to the light and he lowered his arm, he saw the crew staring at him, a respect, and maybe a little fear, in their eyes which had not been there before.

Even Wallace Troy looked at him as if he were seeing someone he didn't know. "How—what did you do?" he asked, his voice tinged with awe.

Josiah looked at Troy coldly, then walked to his cabin. The little room reeked of rum from the glass that had fallen from the table. But the bottle had not been hurt. Josiah picked it up. He stared at it a moment, then, going back on deck, he threw the bottle as far as he could, watching as it made a small splash on the silent sea and then sank.

2

Amina did not know how she had come to be with child. She and Menyu, her husband, had not known each other since her blood-time, which had stopped only a few days before the chalk-faced ones came. They had killed Menyu and her father, the two falling next to each other near the *toguna*, the house of words. Menyu was already dead when she reached them, but she heard a moan from her father and crawled to where he lay. She held him on her lap, his life's blood pouring out of his body like water from a bucket with too many holes.

When he reached up and pulled her face down to his, she thought he was going to whisper some secret in her ear, one that only he as *hogon*, the spiritual leader of their people, would know, a secret which would die with him if he did not tell anyone. Instead, he kissed her full and hard on the mouth, something he had never done, and she felt his last breath go from his body into hers. The warm moisture of his kiss had not evaporated from her lips before a chalk-faced one grabbed her and took her away.

She had kept her tears to herself until she lay in the darkness of the ship's bottom. Then she wept and moaned with the others who lay there. The sounds never stopped. Someone was always crying, always screaming.

One day, or perhaps it was night, for she could not tell in that darkness, she heard a voice:

I am the child conceived by terror.

She did not understand. There were no children there.

I am the child conceived by terror. It is the terror of all those who lie here, all those who have lain and will lie in the abyss of ships like this one. I am the child conceived by terror.

She felt a rolling motion in her abdomen as if something was swimming inside. Though she had never given birth, she knew: there was a child within her. Knowing she had not been with her husband, nor been violated by one of the chalk-faced ones, though other women of the village had, she did not understand how she could be with child. The more she thought about it, the more she realized there was only one explanation. Her father's kiss. With his last breath, he had put his *nyama* inside her.

Her people believed the life of a person was not in the body but the nyama—the life force. When a person died, as her mother had giving birth to her, the nyama did not. It left the body and was given a new home within a small statue the family would have made and placed outside by the door. The nyama remained part of the household and blessed it with prosperity and health. However, if a statue was not made for the nyama, it would wander through the village, causing divisions between husbands and wives, between children and parents, between the hogon and the people. Peace could not return to a village until the hogon led the orphaned nyama away.

Tears came to her eyes as she thought about Menyu's nyama wandering aimlessly with no one to care for it. And where was the home for the nyama of those whose bodies were thrown into the Great Water over which the ship moved? What would they do without a statue to live in, or a hogon to lead them away? And what did it mean that she now carried her father's nyama, as an actual child?

—

I lay within the body of the woman who was called Amina and I listened to the silences between the beats of hearts that beat no more and the wind in breaths that no longer breathed. I saw with eyes that were only sockets in skulls. Though I was no larger than the twinkle of a star, I already knew that lives did not consist only of what happened during one's brief span of years. No. Each person is the sum of the generations that went before, generations of people whose names have been forgotten, whose faces have sunk below where memory can go. Yet those generations live within everyone, pulsating with each heartbeat and each breath.

I listened to the blood roaring through her body, and within the cacophony I found the memories of her brief sixteen years, the memories of her mother and father, their mother and father, and their mother and father, and on back to unnumbered time when no one counted the risings and settings of the sun and there were no months or years but only Time as broad and without end as the universe.

But as intently as I listened, as arduously as I searched, I could not find the reason why I had been conceived. Neither did her blood tell me where we were being taken nor what I was to do when I got there.

When Amma, the creator god and master of life and death, had Amina's father place me inside the woman, he told me my name was Ekundayo, Sorrow Becomes Joy. Surrounded by sorrow deeper than any sea and wider than any sky, I thought I had been misnamed.

3

As the ship neared Charleston, it occurred to Josiah that he did not have to take the woman with him, whichever one she was. He had told Hannah he would, but he had been drinking rum, bad rum. That stuff could make anybody hear voices. Had he really heard Hannah's voice, or had the blacks made him think he had? If they could conjure up a storm, they could certainly make him think his dead wife was speaking inside his head. What choice did he have but to agree to take the pregnant woman with him? But now, as the Charleston docks came into view, the danger of actually doing what he had promised Hannah was churning in his stomach. What would happen if he did nothing? The woman would be sold and taken away, maybe over into Tennessee or down into Mississippi, and that would be the end of it. Or would it?

But how could he get the woman off the ship without anyone knowing? Stealing another man's property, especially a slave, was a serious crime. If he was caught, he'd be put in prison and maybe even hung. If he knew for sure that it really was Hannah's voice he had heard, he would not have any doubts about what to do. But not being sure, well, maybe that was the point. A choice wasn't difficult if you knew the outcome in advance.

The ship reached Charleston harbor early on the afternoon of a hot day. Josiah sent Troy to tell the investors that their slaves had arrived. The slaves were waiting on deck when the three investors came aboard. While they were pleased with the physical condition of the slaves, they were disappointed again in the numbers. They paid Josiah but made it clear that they'd find another captain for the next voyage they financed.

After the slaves were taken away, Josiah paid his crew. They dispersed quickly to the taverns on Bay Street, where they would find the strong liquor they had been craving for the three months of the voyage as well as the women they had craved even more.

Wallace Troy was the last one to leave the ship.

"I had a word with the investors. It looks like I'm going to be captain the next time this ship sets sail for Africa." He grinned. "I made it clear that I didn't coddle niggers and they wouldn't be disappointed when I returned with so many niggers that they wouldn't all fit on deck."

"I wish you much success," Josiah said, with an irony Wallace missed.

"I know how to manage niggers. But I do have one question for you."

"What might that be, Mr. Troy?"

"What did you tell them heathens that made 'em stop that storm? I've been working on slavers for nigh onto ten years and I never seen anything like it in my life. One minute, we thought we were going to be drowned by rain. The next, the sun was shining from a clear blue sky. What did you tell them?"

"What does it matter, Mr. Troy?" Josiah answered finally, not knowing what else to say.

"I guess it don't, except it's the damnedest thing I've ever seen. I'd like to know the magic words so I could use 'em if I ever got in a tight spot."

Josiah shrugged and said nothing.

"Well, I had to ask, but I didn't think you'd help me out. I don't doubt that you'd be happy if you heard that I'd been killed at sea by a bunch of nigger slaves."

"You do me an injustice. I would never rejoice at another's death, not even yours, Mr. Troy."

"You say. Good luck to you, Captain."

"And to you, Mr. Troy."

Wallace Troy swaggered away, leaving Josiah standing at the bottom of the plank that led down from the ship. After Troy turned a corner and was out of sight, Josiah walked slowly up the plank and onto the deck of the ship.

His heart was beating so fast and loud he was afraid the whole city of Charleston could hear it. If only Hannah would speak to him one time more. Just one time more. He needed to know that hearing her voice in the hold of the ship had not been a delusion, that Hannah remained a part of what was real. But he heard nothing except his own confusion and fear.

How was he going to get a pregnant black woman all the way from there to the island? He would have to find someone going in that general direction who would let him and his "slave" ride along. Then he would have to find a skiff and make his way through the intricate waterways that meandered through the islands until he eventually came to the small one that was his. He didn't think he could make that journey with a black woman without getting stopped somewhere along the way by a constable.

The most he could do was get the woman off the boat. Maybe he could get her into the hands of some of the free blacks in Charleston. They would know what to do with her. He had heard there were churches where free blacks worshipped. He'd find one and leave her there. That was best!

He went to his cabin and stuffed his few belongings into his old bag, then hurried down the gangplank and onto the dock. He started walking away when he heard a baby crying. He stopped. There was only silence. He began walking. The baby's cry came again. Josiah stopped. Again, there was only silence. However, this time, as he started moving away, the cry of the baby came again, but this time there was also a strong gust of wind that pushed him back toward the ship. Josiah tried walking against the wind but it grew stronger and the baby's cry became louder. Josiah stopped. The wind and the baby's cry stopped.

Could it have been the baby that called up the storm during the voyage? Josiah wondered.

As if the silent question had been heard, there came a wind so strong that it almost knocked Josiah over. Accompanying the wind was a loud rumble of thunder, though the late afternoon sky was clear.

Slowly, reluctantly, Josiah turned around and went

back to the ship. He left his bag on deck and went down into the hold. He stood for a moment until his eyes adjusted to the darkness. He stood hoping to hear Hannah's voice, but there was only the loud silence.

He looked on each tier on which the slaves had lain. When he got to the top one, he saw a dark shape huddled at the farthest corner, her black skin blending well with the darkness. Although he could not make out the features of her face, her eyes stared into his. He looked into those eyes and saw his own loneliness, grief, and terror. He was ashamed of how close he had come to breaking his promise to Hannah. For the first time since Hannah and their child had died, Josiah had a purpose, a reason for being alive.

"I'll be back soon," he whispered, and hurried up the steps and off the ship. As hard as it was to contain his excitement that he was about to do something that might be called noble and good, he walked casually to the livery on Bay Street, where he bought a horse and wagon, and to the milliner's shop further along the street, where he got a dress and shawl.

By the time he returned to the ship, it was almost dark. He went down into the hold. She was waiting for him at the bottom of the stairs. He gave her the dress and shawl. Even though he could scarcely see her in the darkness, he turned his back while she changed out of the stained and dirty garment she'd been wearing.

"I didn't know your size, so I hope it fits all right," he said nervously, forgetting that she could not understand.

Josiah had thought he would hide her beneath a blanket in the back of the wagon, but what if the patrol stopped him? They were out every night to guard against runaway slaves and would want to know why he was hiding a slave woman. But if she rode on the seat, anyone who saw them would assume she was his slave and perhaps think nothing more.

Taking her hand, Josiah led her up from the hold, across the deck, and quickly down the plank and into the wagon he'd left in the shadows of the ship. He lit the kerosene lamp that had come with the horse and wagon and got in front, taking the horse's reins with his left hand, holding the lamp up with his right so he could see where he was going.

Wait!

It was a young man's voice this time, one Josiah did not know.

Where are we going? the voice wanted to know.

"To my home," Josiah spoke aloud. "It is an island far from here." As he spoke he pictured in his mind the simple one-room house he had shared with Hannah, the house he had scarcely seen in the years since she died. He had built it himself in a large field bordered by trees between the still waters of an inlet and a broad river teeming with fish.

—

I could see in Josiah's mind the house near the river. I saw him standing in the doorway of the house, his arm around the waist of a woman almost as tall and gaunt as he was. Her arm was around his waist. Then the picture in

Josiah's mind changed, and I saw a meadow near the house and a mound of dirt. I felt the pain as Josiah's feelings changed from a warm softness to a sharp, cold emptiness.

That will be a safe place.

Only I heard those words, spoken not by the woman, Hannah, but by Amma, who took us there.

———

The next thing Josiah knew, he and Amina were standing outside his house. They both turned and looked into the sky. They thought they heard the sound of wings rustling against the night. But they saw nothing, and then all was quiet.

4

Amina awoke each morning as the sky was changing from its black garb of night to its rosy one of dawn. Quietly she would get out of bed, go outside, stand for a moment, and look across the meadow to the calm waters of the inlet.

She thought for a moment, trying to remember the word Josiah had taught her for what she was seeing. Finally, it came to her. *Wa-ter.* There were so many new words to learn. *River. Grass. Fish. Bed. Pot. Kettle. Peas. Dish. Bowl.* These were important, but they were not enough. She needed the ones to tell Josiah of heartsickness and loneliness and the bleakness that comes when hope is stillborn.

Among her people words were as alive as any man, woman, or child. They had an odor and she could hear what they smelled like. Words spoken by a good person smelled sweet like the aroma of a good meal. Words spoken by an evil person smelled like rotting meat.

That was why so many on the ship had died. The chalk-faced ones did not know how much they stank. The smell of their constant talk drifted down to the bottom of the ship and, like a noxious cloud, choked them to death.

But each day when they were taken on deck, they were silently glad for the presence of the tall, sad-looking chalk-faced one, because when he spoke to them, the air cleared and smelled of coconut oil.

Josiah's words still smelled sweet to Amina, although his voice was high like a screeching bird's. Her people would have said he was out of balance with nature, because he talked in a woman's voice. To cure him, the people would have put on masks and danced and her father would have chanted for many hours. Eventually, whatever was out of balance inside Josiah would have been healed. His voice would have become lower because he was again in harmony with himself and nature.

Amina knew she was not in harmony with anything in this strange land. What more telling sign could there be than that the child within her had not grown, that her breasts were not beginning to swell with milk. What would she do when the child was born and she could not suckle him?

She turned away from the meadow and followed a path between grasses and wildflowers down to the river. There she squatted and, dipping her hands in the cold river, splashed water on her face. Then she stood, looked into the sky, and prayed:

"Amma, accept my morning blessing. My ancestors, accept my morning blessing."

It was a prayer her people had offered to Amma, the creator god, since the beginning of time. But on this particular morning there was more Amina needed to say:

"Amma. I am but a young woman, alive for barely sixteen years. Why am I here in this strange place? I miss the never-ending plains of my home. I miss the hard earth we worked with all our strength to make it give us grain and vegetables and onions. Here, things grow whether you want them to or not. The grasses, weeds, bushes, and trees want to engulf everything.

"Amma. Josiah is a good man, a kind man. He takes care of me. He teaches me his language and each day I learn many new words. But I miss speaking and hearing the words of my language, whose words have the power of your son, Nommo, the god who gave us speech.

"Amma. I miss my people. I am no one without them. Josiah knows how to live as if he is a finger without a hand. I do not. I am a finger who needs her hand, who needs to be next to other fingers, who needs to know that I am part of something other than myself.

"Amma. I am afraid. This child does not move. He does not grow. Is he dead? I fear that he is. If that is so, I have no purpose, no reason to try and live in this land. I have remained alive only because of the child. Give me a sign, Amma, that the child, this remnant of my father, still lives.

"Amma, hear my morning greeting. Nommo, hear my morning greeting. I am lost. Put me back on the path."

Amina's face was wet with tears as she finished. She was not aware of Josiah standing at the head of the path. Every morning he stood there and watched her as she knelt at the river and washed her face and then said her morning prayers. Then afterward she would stare intently at the water.

He wished he knew how to tell her that he knew something of what she was feeling. At least, he thought he did. Her country had been taken from her. Hannah had been his country, and she had been taken from him. Yet he knew it was not the same. As deep as his grief was, Amina's was endless. He, at least, still lived where the land and language were familiar.

If he had not been painfully shy, he would have walked down the path and put his arms gently around her, his affection and touch a reassurance that neither of them was alone. But there were times when a well-meaning embrace could make someone feel more lonely. So Josiah stood and watched. When Amina turned to come back up the path, he moved quickly toward the house so she would not see him.

———

The next morning Amina awoke at the edge of night becoming day. She had expected Amma to appear to her in a dream and say whether her child lived. But she had not dreamed. She knew the truth now. The child she carried was dead. Why should she continue to live when there was nothing to live for?

Having made her decision, her spirit felt lighter than at any time since the awful day the chalk-faced ones had come. She stood for a moment and looked at Josiah asleep in the bed near the door.

"You are a good man," she whispered in her language. She hoped he would not grieve for her as he did for the one who had died. Every evening as day slipped away, she watched him walk out into the meadow in front of the house. She had seen the mound of earth there and the piece of wood shaped like a cross atop it. He had helped her understand that beneath it lay his wife and their child.

She supposed his having another human around these months had been a comfort to him, as his presence had been a comfort to her. But she didn't think she had been there long enough to have made that much of a difference to him. By the next new moon he would scarcely remember her. She went outside, stopped, and looked up at the sky, which seemed to be bleeding with the first tinges of a red dawn.

"Amma. When my nyama leaves my lifeless body, will you show it the way back to my homeland? Perhaps it can find the peace there which it will never know here. Please, Amma. Take my nyama home. This is my request. This is my prayer."

She turned and walked slowly down the path to the river. She didn't squat and wash her face this morning. Instead she took a deep breath, then stepped into the water.

Josiah had felt her standing over him and had awoken, though she did not know it. He had heard her faint whispers but did not know what she said. He waited behind the door and listened to the anguish in her voice as she addressed what he assumed to be her god. When he heard her move away, he went outside. This morning he did not wait at the top of the path but moved down it to be closer to her. When he saw her step into the river he shouted "Amina!" and started running toward her.

She did not turn at the sound of his voice, but waded farther out into the water. The slow-moving river came now to her waist. She kept walking until the muddy bottom began slanting downward. Now the water was at her breasts. In a few more steps the bottom of the river would fall away and she would drop beneath the surface.

"Amina! Amina!" Josiah shouted again as he reached the river's edge and waded in after her. Suddenly, he stopped.

There, downriver, he saw a serpent, deep red like the sky of the sun's first rising, swimming toward Amina. It was half as big around as the river was wide and so long that Josiah could not see its tail. Josiah hurried out of the water and ran quickly up the path to get his rifle from the house.

But when Amina saw the serpent, she smiled for the first time since the chalk-faced ones had taken her away.

"Lebe!" she said softly, closing her eyes, her face shining in prayerful ecstasy as the serpent, the first hogon and god of the earth and all that grew from it, slowly began entwining himself around her.

Josiah rushed from the house, rifle in hand, and ran down the path. He saw the serpent wrapping itself around Amina. He brought the rifle to his shoulder and took aim. As Josiah's index finger started to squeeze the trigger, the upper part of the serpent's body moved so quickly that Josiah wasn't aware even of movement, only that now the serpent's head was directly in front of his own, its forked tongue flicking rapidly in and out of its mouth. Josiah screamed, stumbled backward, and fell to the ground, losing his grip on the weapon. The serpent lowered its body until its head was above Josiah's. He closed his eyes and waited for the serpent to strike him. But nothing happened. When he dared, he opened his eyes slowly.

The serpent's head was so close that Josiah had no choice but to look into its eyes. There, to his surprise, Josiah saw tears as black as the hold of a slave ship. Josiah could have sworn he heard screams and cries coming from the tears. Tears welled in Josiah's eyes and trickled slowly down his face.

As if satisfied by hearing the correct answer to a question Josiah was not aware had even been asked, the serpent returned to Amina.

Around and around her he moved, slowly, and with seemingly no effort. The touch of the serpent against Amina's skin was less than that of a feather, and she relaxed into Lebe's embrace. *Amma has sent Lebe to take me home,* she thought. Amina closed her eyes more tightly, and her smile widened as she awaited the tensing of Lebe's muscles and the squeeze that would take the breath from her body.

But the serpent seemed to be taking great care to show her its tenderness as it moved slowly, gently, its body now like a soft wind against her skin.

Time passed and Amina waited for that deep sleep she imagined death to be. But instead of sinking into the darkness of death, Amina felt a breath on her cheek. Could it be? Was there someone else in the dark and feathered redness? Yes. There was, and whoever this person was embraced her. She would have never imagined that death would come with such love, and she relaxed into the arms holding her.

Then a quiet masculine voice spoke in the language of her people:

"Thank you for bringing me safely across the Great Water."

Amina opened her eyes and looked up to see the black face, soft eyes, and smiling lips of a young man who looked like her father must have looked when he was young.

"I am Ekundayo," he continued.

"I am not dead?"

"No, and I hope you will not be for many years to come."

Amina did not understand. How could this young man have come from her body? She had felt no pain, no feeling that anything was leaving her body. Who was he? Whoever he was, he was not like a normal man born from a woman. Ekundayo was no child that needed a mother's breast and protection. When he had announced himself to her in the bottom of the ship, he had called himself a seed. She had not carried a child but merely a seed that Lebe had brought forth as a young man.

Now what? She knew she should be happy, but she had been prepared to die in the hope that her nyama would return home. But she was alive. She looked up into Ekundayo's face and saw that he had no need of her. His eyes were quiet and confident like her father's had been. It was obvious; her task here was finished. Her desire to return to her home was stronger than ever. But how could she get Lebe to take her nyama there?

Just then, there came a woman's voice, a voice high-pitched and nasal like Josiah's, the same voice she had heard on the slave ship when it spoke to Josiah.

It is not your time, the voice said. *You are needed here.*

Amina gave a short, harsh laugh. *No one needs me.*

I do, the woman's voice said in return.

Why would you need me?

I need you to be the resting place of my spirit.

"That is impossible," Amina said aloud this time. "A person cannot be the resting place for the nyama of a dead one."

How can you be sure?

Amina had to admit that she couldn't be, not after all that had happened. Last year, on her wedding day, if someone had told her that chalk-faced ones would kill Menyu and her father, and carry her to a place she had never known existed, she would have said that was impossible.

In this land where it seemed that people did not know about nyama, did not know statues needed to be made in which nyama could live once they left the body, perhaps nyama had no choice but to take up residence in the bodies of living people.

Are you the nyama of Josiah's wife? Amina asked silently.

Yes. I am Hannah came the response.

Amina did not understand how she could be the resting place for the nyama of someone who was not of her people. But, with sadness, she realized a truth she did not want to accept: she no longer had a people. Though only six full moons had passed since she had been at Josiah's, memories of her people and her village had begun to fade.

As much as she did not want to accept that she would never see her village again, she knew that was the truth. Even if Amma made it possible for her to return, her village would not be the same. So many had been killed, so many taken away. Her village did not exist anymore, except as fragments of memory. Was she, too, only a fragment now?

"That depends on you," Ekundayo answered, as if he had been listening to her thoughts.

"What do you mean?" she wanted to know.

"We must begin again, all of us the chalk-faced ones have brought here, all the ones that are to come. We must create ourselves anew."

"How do I do that?"

Receive me came Hannah's high voice.

"But I already have an nyama. How can I receive the nyama of another?" Amina spoke aloud, addressing her question to Ekundayo as if she would only believe what he would tell her.

There was a long silence before Ekundayo finally spoke. "I do not know," he said. "There is much I do not understand about this land. It is far larger than you could ever imagine and it is filled with nyama of the dead who are not cared for. These nyama have more power than the living and they goad the living to do violence and cultivate hatred as if it were corn seed."

He was silent again, but this time it was as if he was listening to something, or someone. "Hannah says that if you will be her resting place, she will not harm your nyama. Instead, she will share with it all she knows—how to cook and make clothes as she did, the songs and stories she knows, her memories, everything you need to know to live here."

Amina was afraid to say yes. Then she thought of Josiah, thought of how she had hid in the darkest corner of the ship's hold waiting for him to come for her. She remembered how afraid she had been that he would not keep his promise, how afraid that he would leave her there, alone and forgotten. But he had come. She remembered smelling his fear and how she had wept when he went away. But he had returned, and he had turned his back when she undressed to put on the dress he had brought her. How afraid had he been to take her into his life? But, afraid, he had said yes.

So Amina closed her eyes again, took a deep breath and let it out slowly.

I will receive your nyama.

No sooner had she thought the words than she gasped audibly as a warmness went up and down her body. At that moment Lebe uncoiled and slipped back into the river.

Josiah had remained on the ground, and only now, as he saw the serpent vanish, did he get up slowly, to see Amina and a young black man, almost as tall as Josiah, beside her.

"Josiah!" Amina called excitedly as she and Ekundayo left the water. "I want you to meet my son."

"Amina! Amina! You spoke to me in English."

She hadn't realized it until Josiah told her. "I did, didn't I?" she said tentatively, relieved that her voice was still her own.

"I'm proud to meet you," Josiah said, walking down the sloping path, his hand extended.

As Ekundayo moved forward to shake Josiah's hand, he stopped, gasped, and then began screaming loudly. It was a cry so loud and so filled with anguish and pain that it seemed to be coming up from the earth beneath his feet, into his body, and out through his mouth. Over and over the scream came until his body sagged. Josiah caught him as he slumped to the ground.

5

Though my eyes were closed and I appeared to be unconscious, I was not. I was aware when the one called Josiah picked me up, carried me to the house, and laid me on a bed. I was aware of Josiah and Amina's concerns, their helplessness at not knowing what to do as I rolled and twisted from side to side, sweat pouring from my body as if I were being boiled from within.

But regardless of how I turned, they kept coming—men, women, and children—erupting from the earth and pouring down from a wide gash in the blue fabric of the sky. Some hopped on one leg, the stump of the absent leg showing the gashes of shark teeth. Others had no legs and propelled themselves forward on strong arms. Some were missing arms, while others had wounds from which blood poured without stopping. Still others carried their heads in the crooks of arms, the mouths in the heads opening and closing as if there was something they needed to say, but no sound came out.

The maimed figures looked like people, except their bodies were transparent, as if made of fog. They filled every inch of the room, standing in neat rows and staring down at me from the dark hollows in their faces where eyes used to be. I could hear Amina and Josiah talking about me, but they were unaware of the nyama standing all around them staring at me in the nakedness of a need I did not understand.

Finally, sleep came, but it was not the sweet blackness that provided refuge from cares and anxieties. This darkness was like that which existed before Amma created the world. But as I descended into it, there was none of the delicate softness of that darkness from which Amma emerged to bring life into the world.

The darkness in which I found myself was where Time had gathered up the wounds people inflicted on each other. Humans would not know how to live if they remembered the evil they did. So Time kept the wounds in a darkness rife with the pain of evil, a pain I felt as I descended deeper and deeper into Time's memory.

I wondered why I was being subjected to this pain, but Time knew who I was and why Amma had brought me to this land, and Time told me that my destiny was to heal the wounds, something I could not do without knowing the pain. So she released memories of evil she had been keeping like precious heirlooms. Like great birds bringing winds from the caves where they slept at the four corners of the earth, the memories came and I was carried deeper and deeper into the darkness made hard by the pain of evil.

I saw chalk-faced Soul Stealers and black-faced Soul Stealers going into villages and taking people away in chains. The Soul Stealers took swords and thrust them deep into the bowels of any who resisted, took swords and sliced off the heads of any who dared fight back. Some-times the Soul Stealers killed others for the sheer pleasure that having the power of life and death gave them.

I did not want to see more, but Time needed me to. I saw captured blacks put onto ships like the one that had brought Amina and me to this land. Their number stretched to the four horizons, more than I could have ever counted. But Time remembered each one individually as well as the dreams that died the moment they were taken into the holds of the ships, the memories of freedom they dared not cling to, the pictures in their minds of the land and lives that would never be theirs again.

Time also held, as if they were as valuable as dia-monds, the memories of those who were killed and those who died in the holds of the ships. I saw rose-colored cir-cles, which looked to be made from clouds, leave their bodies. These were their nyama and they followed the cap-tured ones onto the ships and into the holds. Like silence dancing, the nyama floated before the faces of the cap-tured ones, needing to be recognized and cared for. But the captured ones could not see the nyama because of the tears in their eyes and the terror in their hearts. The nyama did not understand why statues were not being carved for them to live in, now that the bodies in which they had resided no longer held them. Would there be no one ask-ing for their help in the many trials the gods subjected a person to?

When the nyama realized they were not going to be taken care of, they mourned the death of the bond be-tween past and present, spirit and body, existence and emptiness. As they mourned, their rosiness turned a dark red, and in despair they settled onto the beams, pallets, and floors of the slave ships.

But as the voyages continued, the nyama wondered what horror they had entered, as captured ones, dead and alive, were tossed into the ocean. The nyama fleeing those bodies flung into the water did not look like any Time had ever embraced; some were misshapen gray circles with holes like bug-eaten fabric. Others were flat, like metal that had been beaten into thin sheets. Yet others were only a little larger than small stones and just as hard.

Up from the depths of Time's memory came questions, questions for which Time had no answers: What happened when no one was left to make a home for the nyama? What happened when no one remembered that nyama existed and needed the love of the living? What happened when nyama were so damaged by the suffering inflicted on those in whom they had lived that they became angry and wanted to inflict suffering on the living?

I writhed against the pain. Sweat poured from my body and I clenched my hands into fists so tight that the nails of my fingers pierced the palms. I gasped, aware only dimly that Amina was wiping the perspiration from my body while Josiah wet my lips with cool water.

Finally, the memories ceased coming. I felt myself being lifted out of the tortured blackness and up into a blinding light from a blood-red sun. The light was so bright I brought up my arm to shield my eyes even though they were closed. That did not make a difference. Then from out of the light flew a great bird of death-black feathers, and the bird spoke to me in a small, frightened voice:

"I am Amma, the god who created all, the god who is the master of life and death. I am a god, but I am afraid. The chalk-faced Soul Stealers do not understand what they are doing. They think they are bringing people here only to do their labor. But they have released forces they have no knowledge of, forces they cannot control. Their ignorance and cruelty threaten the very fabric of creation.

"This land is filled with millions of nyama, those of all the blacks taken from their lands, those who died in the bottoms of the ships, those thrown into the Great Water, and those who have died here without knowing even that they had an nyama. But this land also holds nyama of people who exist only in the fragments of place-names the ignorant chalk-faced ones have retained: Omaha. Iowa. Connecticut. Dakota. I never knew that names could become stones marking the graves of the dead.

"This is a land in which death is more important than life. The Soul Stealers fill the air with nyama and do not know that so many nyama without a place to be, without people to care for them, can cause the heavens to fall into the chaos that existed before I ordered sun to number the days.

"Something must be done before it is too late. That is why I have brought you to this land. You must find a resting place for the nyama before they destroy everything, and even I will be lost in the flood of destruction."

"What must I do?" I asked, though my lips had not moved.

"I do not know" came the sad response. "I do not know."

And then all was silent. The great bird flew into the blood-red light, and as the light faded I found myself descending again into the darkness. I struggled against going, but Time said she needed to show me my origin.

I saw a village where fierce fighting was going on between blacks and Soul Stealers. A young man and an older one were desperately chanting a prayer, one calling forth nyama to come to their aid. And they did, rising from the statues sitting beside the entrance to each home, rosy, cloudlike, snake-curved figures. The Soul Stealers did not see and did not feel the nyama enter their bodies through their nostrils, mouths, and ears, but suddenly the Soul Stealers began to cry out as they struggled to breathe. They did not know that their nyama were being killed by the nyama of the village. One by one, the Soul Stealers began falling to the ground, more dead than dead because their nyama died with them.

The people of the village with the help of the nyama were on the verge of defeating the Soul Stealers until one with dirty yellow hair and a scraggly beard raised the long stick he was carrying. He did not know why his men were dying though no one had struck them. He thought it might have something to do with the young man and the old one and the words they were chanting. The Soul Stealer raised the stick, pointed it at the older of the two men. The stick made a loud noise and the older man fell to the ground. As the younger man turned in the direction of the sound, another Soul Stealer came from behind and thrust a sword through his body with such force that I could see the sword's point coming out of the young man's abdomen.

The chanting stopped and almost immediately the nyama left the bodies of the Soul Stealers, and, like kites whose strings had been broken, they drifted skyward.

A young woman screamed as she ran to the body of the younger man. It was Amina. She screamed again but, hearing a moan, she turned and saw the older man lying nearby. She crawled to him and took him in her arms.

I saw the older man's nyama begin separating from his body. This nyama was neither snake-curved nor round but was like a giant serpent. From that I understood: the dying man was a hogon. His nyama would be that of the very first hogon—Lebe, a son of Amma.

Lebe was almost free of the hogon's body when out of the sky came a giant bird of night-black feathers. Amma! The bird fell onto Lebe. The giant serpent writhed and struggled, but Amma was stronger and forced Lebe back inside the hogon's body. The hogon knew what Amma wanted him to do and he reached up, grasped Amina's face between the palms of his hands, and, opening his mouth, kissed her. My eyes widened as I saw Lebe stream from the body of the hogon and into Amina's. Then, the hogon fell backward, dead.

While tears streamed down Amina's face, a struggle was taking place inside her, as Lebe coupled with Amina's nyama and from the coupling came a round cloudlike circle shining with a soft red light. That was my nyama, and just before Amma flew away, he whispered my name— Ekundayo.

At long last, Time relaxed her grasp on me and I floated up and out of her darkness. As I relaxed into the honey-soft blackness of sleep, I heard Time weeping with quiet joy. She was no longer alone with her memories.

6

I slept for five days. On the morning of the sixth, I awoke. I was afraid to open my eyes, afraid I would see nyama still pouring from the bowels of earth and the vault of heaven.

Finally, I took a deep breath, let it out slowly, and opened my eyes. The nyama were still there, filling every space in the room. I looked up and through the ceiling and saw nyama filling the sky.

It was strange to see nyama in the form of the bodies in which they had lived. I searched through my memory, which now contained not only the lives and memories of every hogon, including Lebe, but also the memories Time had given me. But in none of them could I find nyama who looked like pale imitations of the flesh they had occupied. Perhaps in this land nyama had been forced to look like their bodily selves in hopes a few people would see them and understand; death killed only the body.

A young man stepped out of the crowd of nyama by the bed on which I lay. In his abdomen was a large hole. I recognized him: his name was Menyu. He, with the hogon, had chanted and called out the nyama to fight the Soul Stealers. The nyama in the room parted and allowed

Menyu's to cross the room and stand next to the bed where Amina lay sleeping. He looked down at her and then at me.

I knew immediately what he wanted me to do.

When first light made the hem of the sky turn pale, I got up very slowly, as my body ached from having lain in bed so long. But that did not matter. I had work to do.

I looked around the room and saw a large knife lying on the fireplace hearth. I took it and went quietly outside. Seeing the path, I made my way down to the river.

There, as if someone had known I would be coming, I found three pieces of wood, each about three feet in length, laid out neatly in a row. The wood was soft, which made it easy to cut. My hand felt it was being guided by other hands, unseen ones, that knew how to transform wood into a being. A head began to emerge from the wood as I carved into it. As I worked, I wondered if I was little more than wood to Amma, who was carving me into the shape he wanted me to be.

I felt rather than saw the presences of Amina and Josiah standing at the mouth of the path, looking down at me. If I looked up, I knew they would come to exclaim their happiness that I was awake, that I was alive. But I did not look at them. I had to finish carving at least one of the figures.

The sun had begun its descent from the top of the sky when the statue was completed. It was the figure of a man. His head was shaped like a thin oval, the body long, with a protruding belly and slender legs. The figure rested on a flat pedestal, which would allow it to stand.

I looked at the figure, turning it around slowly, not admiring it so much as inspecting it. Satisfied, I got up slowly and started up the path toward Josiah and Amina.

———

Amina gasped when she saw what Ekundayo carried in his hands. Tears poured down her face when he held the figure out to her. She took it with trembling hands and clasped it to her bosom. Ekundayo took her in his arms and held her tightly as she sobbed for her young husband, her body heaving as her pain poured out.

When her crying finally ebbed and then stopped, she took the figure and placed it on the right side of the doorway to the cabin. Then she and Ekundayo began chanting:

Oh, your head is fallen!
Good is the way to the right,
Evil is the way to the left.
Dead one, may God Amma set you on the correct path,
May Amma lead you by his strong hand.

Over and over they chanted. After a while, another voice joined theirs, one high and thin but strong. His sense of the melody was true, and after a while, he had learned the words. Though he did not understand their meaning, he understood the body-wracked sobs that broke into Amina's singing. And so the three of them sang the funeral song for Menyu, Amina's slain husband, as the sun made its way slowly down the sky.

When the sun began to lie down in the well of night, Ekundayo saw Menyu's pale nyama come out of the house and hover above the carved figure. After staring at it for a long moment, the nyama disappeared into it.

Ekundayo's voice became stronger and louder as he changed the melody from the slow and mournful one they had sung all afternoon into one that was still melancholy but faster in tempo and lighter in tone:

Dead one, may God Amma set you on the correct path.
May Amma lead you by his strong hand.

Amina's face brightened as she understood that the nyama of her murdered husband had entered his resting place. His spirit was there now to protect her. She hurried into the house and returned with a handful of rice. Slowly she poured it over the statue.

"Welcome, my husband. And be at peace," she said softly. "Welcome. And be at peace."

The next day Ekundayo carved figures for Amina's father and for Josiah's child. The same ritual was repeated. This time Josiah knew all the words, and his voice had settled more into his chest and he sang with almost the same strength as Ekundayo and Amina.

That night they sat quietly at the table in the cabin, tired but happy. Josiah felt like he had a hundred questions, but his ignorance of what had transpired was so great he didn't know what to ask or even how. Finally, he uttered a name. "Hannah?" he said, wondering why a statue had been made for his child but not his wife.

In the dim light from the candles he saw Ekundayo's eyes shift toward Amina. Josiah looked at her, gasped, and started to say something. Ekundayo shook his head. "Do not ask anymore about it," he said firmly.

Josiah closed his mouth, but his heart beat with a rhythm and liveliness it had not had since Hannah's death. He wondered if he would ever understand all he had seen and experienced since Hannah's voice had spoken to him in the hold of the ship. He doubted it, because everything defied explanation. He had been looked at by a serpent who saw into the shadowed recesses of his soul, a serpent who had coiled itself around Amina without crushing her, a serpent who had transformed the seed in Amina's womb into a young man.

If that were not enough, there were the changes in Amina. She emerged from the serpent's embrace speaking English as if she had spoken it all her life. And there were the moments when she looked at him with a soft, shy smile and then lowered her eyes, and Josiah could've sworn he had seen Hannah. That was impossible, of course. But maybe his view of what was and was not possible was too small.

He had grown up believing in what he could see with his eyes and touch with his hands. He believed in God, of course, but as a remote figure somewhere in a vague place called heaven. Amina's world, however, was comprised of unseen but powerful forces that ignored what he thought of as real. She and Ekundayo accepted as normal what Josiah would have thought impossible.

—

The next morning when Amina and Josiah awoke, Ekundayo lay on the floor, dead.

PART TWO

1

Nat? Are you all right?"

At the sound of the voice, I opened my eyes, startled. I lay still, blinking as I tried to awake from a sleep so deep I felt I was trying to come back from the dead. I knew I had been dreaming, but all I could remember was that I had been flying through the night.

I looked up at the weathered boards of the ceiling. It was a moment before I realized something was wrong. Before I had gone to sleep I had looked up at a ceiling made from logs!

"Did you hear me, Nat?" came the woman's voice again from the other side of the room.

Who was that? It did not sound like Amina or Josiah, the only two people I knew. And who was Nat?

"Say something! I heard you cry out in your sleep."

I was surprised when my mouth opened and a voice, higher in tone than my normal deeper and softer one, came from inside me and said, "I'm all right, Grandmama."

I knew *I* had not spoken, but the unfamiliar voice had come from my chest.

"Maybe a witch was riding you," the woman responded. "They be out looking for folks to bedevil on nights when the full moon be shining as bright as it was last night. I ain't never seen a moon as big and bright as that one. Must've been some ha'nts or spirits moving about last night." She sighed. "Well, I got to get to the big house. I won't be needing you in the kitchen this morning. Master Chelsea is in Charleston at some meeting. Miss Ellen's still in Richmond with Master Gregory's mother. I got to start getting the house ready for the wedding."

In my mind I saw an old woman, small and thin with short, graying hair. Her shoulders were stooped and rounded, as if her life had become too heavy to carry. Her name was Harriet, and she was the cook for the slave owner's family. But how did I know all that?

"Don't you sleep too long," Harriet said, going out the door.

I sat up and looked around. The room was smaller than the one of Josiah's cabin. There was a fireplace against the rear wall; a small but well-made table and two chairs sat in front of the hearth. Against the wall opposite me was the bed where Harriet slept.

I looked at the furniture and felt a swelling of pride inside me, as if I had made the table, chairs, and bed frames. But I hadn't. That much I was sure of. Yet the feeling of pride reasserted itself, insisting that I had made them.

Outside I heard doors opening and closing, and the sounds of people greeting each other. Suddenly, the door of the cabin opened, and a girl came hurrying in. She was almost as tall and black in color as I was. She had a small, round face with eyes that would have been laughter if they could have made a sound. Around her head was tied a white cloth. Her face brightened into a wide grin when she looked at me. She closed the door, flung herself into my arms, and kissed me softly but passionately on the lips.

Her name was Sylvie, but I didn't understand how I knew that, and why she was kissing me. Unless. There was only one explanation that made sense. I must not look like Ekundayo any longer. I must look like the one Harriet called Nat.

"What's the matter with you this morning?" Sylvie asked. She was annoyed with me, I guess, because I had not returned her kiss or put my arms around her. "Something wrong?"

"I think a witch must've been riding me last night," that other voice said.

"Don't surprise me. When I looked at that moon last night, it gave me the creeps. I knew witches, ha'nts, and all kinds of spirits would be out. They need the moonlight to see by. When I saw Sister Harriet walking to the big house and you wasn't with her, I wondered if something was the matter, and I said my honey must not be feeling too good this morning. He could probably use a little sugar from Sylvie." She laughed. "If you put a sieve by your bed tonight, when the witch comes, she'll step in the sieve and her days using you for her horse will be over."

I knew some kind of response was expected, but all I could manage was a weak smile.

"Walk me to the field?" Sylvie asked.

I could not do anything until I understood what had happened to me. "I don't feel too well."

Sylvie eyed me suspiciously. "That witch wouldn't be named Miss Ellen, would it?" she asked angrily. "You been acting different ever since New Year's, when Master Chelsea had that big party for her. I be glad when she's married and moves to the Foster plantation, even though that ain't far enough. Maybe when she's gone, you'll act like black Sylvie is good enough for you."

I didn't know who Ellen was, but a warmth went through my body at the mention of her name.

Sylvie looked at me, waiting for a response, waiting, I suppose, for Nat to tell her what she needed to hear, but I had no idea what that might be. I was sorry when I saw tears come into her eyes.

"Just forget I said anything. Forget I was here this morning. Forget you even know my name!" And she ran out, slamming the door behind her.

I slumped to the floor beside the bed. What had happened? Last night I was Ekundayo. I remembered falling asleep on the floor, strangely comforted by the sound of Josiah's snoring. But now I was Nat, a slave, with a grandmother named Harriet, and a girlfriend named Sylvie. A voice told me I also had a father named Gabriel and a mother named Lizzie. She had died giving birth to Nat, and he had been raised by Harriet, the mother of his mother.

I asked the voice who Miss Ellen was, and how had I, Ekundayo, come to occupy the body of someone named Nat, whose voice had been speaking from within me? The voice did not respond.

I knew the answer to my questions lay somewhere in Time's memory. But was it possible for me to go into that vast memory on my own, or did I have to wait for Time to come and take me? Not knowing what else to do, I closed my eyes and looked into the darkness.

At first I saw only a blackness, then suddenly I was plunging into that blackness, but not as deep into it as before, because the blackness opened and I saw myself asleep on the floor in Josiah and Amina's cabin. I watched, fascinated, as a small cloud of perfect roundness, glowing pink and red as if a sun lived within it, floated slowly out of my sleeping body. Nyama left people's bodies as they slept each night. What people thought of as dreams was what their nyama were seeing and experiencing on their nightly excursions backward and forward in time and through other dimensions. However, there was the danger that an nyama would become so involved in what it was doing that it would forget to return to the body in which it belonged before dawn. If that happened, the body died. As I watched my nyama float up to the ceiling, I wondered if it had failed to return to my body in time.

My nyama was about to go through the ceiling and into the night air when Amma, in the likeness of a giant bird, the same giant bird of night-black feathers that had forced Lebe back into the body of Amina's father, came through the roof without making a sound or even a hole. He grabbed my nyama with his talons, then spread his great wings and rose up and through the roof, leaving behind my soon-to-be-dead body.

———

The great bird flew rapidly through the night, his talons holding tightly to Ekundayo's nyama. The full moon shone big and white as Amma flew from South Carolina to Virginia. Many people swore they saw a shadow across the face of the moon. Some said it was the Angel of Death, the same one that had slain the firstborn of Egypt when Pharaoh refused to free the children of Israel. Sheep's blood on the doorposts of the Israelites' homes had kept the Angel of Death from killing any of their firstborn. No one who saw Amma flying across the face of the moon that night had sheep's blood, but all those who could find a string of garlic to nail to their doors did so. Those who couldn't prayed God would turn His wrath away from them and those they loved.

Amma was too intent on his mission to know what those below were thinking as they saw his desperate flight. The nyama he clutched in his talons was his only hope to save this country, its people, and even himself. But he had to put the nyama into its new body before the sun cleared the eastern horizon, or the nyama would not be fit for any body and would join all the other orphaned nyama with which this land teemed.

Even a god can tire, especially if he does not often assume the form of a bird and fly hundreds of miles through the night air beneath the chill of a full moon. Amma was breathing hard, and his wings were so heavy he could scarcely keep them moving.

Just as blackness began recoiling from the oncoming light of day, he saw the cabin where a young man slept whose name was Nat. Though he was yet young, he had refused the challenge of life. His nyama was weak, and he was going to die soon of a broken heart.

Now he will live, Amma thought, as he dropped with great speed from the apex of darkness and through the roof of the cabin. He thrust Ekundayo's nyama into Nat's chest. Nat sat up and screamed out in horror. But even before the scream ended, the bird was flying up and through the roof.

Amma flew into the deepest part of the forest that surrounded the plantation, a place so thick with trees that the sun scarcely ever penetrated it. There, next to a large and bottomless lake, he perched on a high and strong limb and was immediately asleep. All the other birds in the forest flew away. So great was their fear of a bird so large who slept while the sun was awake that no birds are seen in that place even to this day.

—

I did not know how to believe all I was shown. I had been startled enough when the nyama of Josiah's dead wife became part of Amina. But this was even more unsettling. The nyama of someone living—me—had been placed in another living person, the one named Nat. This was against the order of things.

But I was not sure if I knew what the order of things was anymore. There seemed to be a new order that called for blacks to be carried across the Great Water and made into slaves, an order which Nat already knew, an order which Amma wanted me to learn so I could keep the nyama from destroying the world. But before I could do that, and it was not certain I could, I had to learn all I could about Nat, whose body I now occupied.

I focused my attention and energy on my abdomen.

This was where nyama resided. I saw the perfect circle of rosiness. Next to it was a long, thin wisp that looked like smoke from a dying fire. It was so thin in places I could see through it.

I did not want to believe that what I was seeing was Nat's nyama. Everyone's nyama was a perfect circle of rosiness when they were born. How they lived with the inevitable suffering life brought could change the color, shape, and even substance of their nyama. Even though Nat was a slave, his nyama should not have looked as if it could be blown away by a heavy sigh. What had happened to him? What had he done or not done that his nyama had less substance than a passing thought? His nyama was so fragile it would not have sustained the boy's life for more than another month or two at most.

I knew what I had to do, even though doing it would probably destroy Nat's nyama. But I had no choice. Nat did not have long to live anyway, and everything I needed to know was in his nyama. As I was trying to figure out how to take the knowledge I needed from the boy's nyama, it began pouring all it knew into me. It was as if Nat recognized that his one chance to be remembered lay in the nyama which had been put into his body.

Thus, I learned how Nat walked and talked, how he smiled, what he found funny, the foods he liked, his knowledge of woods and tools and how to build fences, chairs, bureaus, barns, and houses, as well as the faces and names of the people on the plantation.

Then from Time's memory came the knowledge of events Nat had not known he had, memories bequeathed him when Lizzie, his mother, held him in her arms for the few minutes she'd lived after his birth. There was the memory of Gabriel, his father, standing outside the cabin where Lizzie, whom he loved more than life itself, was dying as she birthed his son, and Harriet coming to the door to tell him that Lizzie was dead and she had given birth to a son, his son, whom Harriet was not going to let him see, and she told him if he ever came near the boy, she would try her best to get Master Chelsea to sell him so far into slavery nobody would find him even if freedom came. There also came memories Harriet had given Nat as she held him and kissed his tiny lips, memories she had not known she was giving him, but memories do not have to be known to exist. Thus, I saw all that Harriet had ever seen and all she had heard and everything she knew from having lived as a slave on the Chelsea plantation in Virginia from the instant she first took a breath.

Memories flowed from Time like the roaring rapids of an unnavigable river roiling through a gorge: Nat as a child helping Harriet in the kitchen of the big house, his being taken into a building where an old slave with hair as white and knotted as frost on grass in December patiently chipped away at a large piece of wood and, with awe in his eyes, Nat watching as the wood took the shape of a chair. The old man, whose name was Fulani, had died just months before, but not before teaching the boy how to build fences, barns, houses, and furniture, as well as how to transform pieces of wood into birds and faces and animals.

Finally, the memories ceased flowing into me from

Nat's nyama. I saw that my nyama was bigger and wider than it had been. To my surprise, Nat's nyama still existed, even though it had shrunk until it was scarcely as long as the space between a man's steps. There must have been some memory Nat had withheld from me. I could think of no other reason why this remnant of his nyama still existed. Then I remembered: Ellen! Nat's nyama had not shown me anything about her. Why? I waited, thinking that my knowing what he had withheld would force him to give me his memories of her. Nothing came.

I opened my eyes. I was breathing heavily and drenched in sweat.

What now? I asked silently. What now?

2

Over the next few days I learned that pretending to be Nat was easier than I would have imagined. The boy did not talk a lot, nor show much emotion. However, in that shred of the boy's nyama that remained, I sensed a deep sadness. Was Ellen the cause of the sadness? Why was he not telling me anything about her? But perhaps he could not tell me because he had not told himself. Was that why he was so quiet around others? Was he using his energy to hide feelings he did not want others, including himself, to know he had?

I felt that I came closest to touching the boy's heartsong when I was working in the carpentry shed. It was a two-room building next to the blacksmith's shed at the outer edge of the plantation. The front room was reserved for painting, lacquering, and polishing finished pieces of furniture, doors, window sashes, and the like. The back and larger room contained wood, saws, sawhorses, carving tools, and a long worktable.

Along the back wall of that room I found a long wooden box. When I opened it I was surprised to find inside canes with heads like birds, canes in the shapes of serpents, and statues of animals with the faces of birds and bodies of lions. They had been carefully carved, smoothed, and lacquered to a high sheen. I knew they had been made by Fulani—even if Nat's memory had not told me—because they reminded me so painfully of home. I held each one, gently, lovingly, as if I were holding not an object but Fulani's memories of gods and life in a place he knew he would never see again.

I was sorry Nat's teacher was dead. If we had met, the two of us would have eased each other's loneliness, a loneliness and despair I knew Fulani had suffered, especially when I opened a small trunk hidden deep in the shadows beneath the worktable. Inside were carved statues almost identical to the ones I had made for Josiah and Amina.

I took each one out and stood it on the floor. There were twenty-five of them. It was clear to me they were meant to be for nyama of the dead. No other statues looked quite like those carved for nyama. I wondered if Amma had brought Fulani here and asked him to find a resting place for the nyama of the dead. But Fulani had failed, and, looking at the statues he had carved, I knew why. He had not lavished on the statues the love and care he had put into the canes. To care for nyama, one had to love the dead as much as one loved life. But Fulani had tried. And perhaps in this land the nyama did not know their home was supposed to be in such carved figures. What I had done for the nyama of Amina's father and husband and Josiah's child could not be done for the nyama of this violent and brutal land. There had to be another way, a new way, to give the nyama peace. But if Amma did not know what it was, how was I?

As I started to return the statues to the trunk, I saw, at the bottom, something wrapped neatly in a white cloth. I took it out and carefully unfolded the cloth. Inside was a statue of a woman clothed in nothing but her beauty, and beautiful she was, standing tall, her arms outstretched, her head flung back, long hair streaming down her back like light from heaven. The statue had been carefully polished and then lacquered until it was as smooth and soft to the touch as a morning in early spring. As I held it, my body was filled with an expansive warmth so intense that beads of perspiration broke out on my forehead. But beneath the warmth was such sadness that tears came into my eyes. As I placed the statue back on the white cloth and rewrapped it, my body became filled with grief, as if it were Nat himself who was being put back into hiding.

In the front room was a chest of drawers on the table awaiting another coat of finish. It was a large piece of furniture with four drawers. On the face of each drawer, a carving stood out from the wood as if born there. On the bottom drawer was a row of sunflowers. The third was alive with the broad wings of a large hawk whose beak looked alive enough that it could bite. The second drawer held the profile of a young woman with long hair, a small nose and mouth, and eyes so large that, even in wood, they were filled with an eager hunger for anything and all that life might offer. I was certain this was the same woman as the statue hidden at the bottom of the trunk in the back room.

The top drawer showed two clasped hands. I did not have to look at "my" hands to know that the carved one on the left was Nat's. I could only assume that the chest of drawers was for Ellen, and the carvings were to remind her of experiences she had shared with Nat.

As I began applying a coat of finish to the chest of drawers, I found that I was afraid. I did not want to become entangled in Nat's emotions. Amma had brought me to this place to bring peace to the nyama.

What I did not understand was if, in the meantime, I was supposed to live Nat's life. But I did not want the life of a slave. The very idea that someone could own me and did was enough to make me want to kill.

And there was Ellen. The beauty Nat had put into the statue and the chest of drawers was all the evidence I needed to know that the emotions Nat clung to in the leftover piece of his nyama were about Ellen, the slave master's daughter. What would happen to me, if and when Nat released all of his love for Ellen into my nyama?

—

"Ain't no good goin' to come of it," Harriet mumbled.

The next morning I was sitting at the kitchen table eating breakfast. I smiled. I had learned that Harriet had a way of pretending that she was talking to herself when her words were really directed at Nat.

"I can feel it like I feel the heat off this cookstove. She be better off not marrying nobody than marrying somebody she don't love. This is all Master Chelsea's doing. He ain't thinking about Ellen. He's thinking about joining his plantation with Master Foster's. And Master Foster is thinking about joining his to Master Chelsea's. I sho hope

Master Gregory got enough love for him and Ellen both, 'cause if he's depending on her love for him, he's gon' be standing in the rain without an umbrella.

"But it's my fault. I never should have let you and her be together so much when you was coming up. You and her would sit right there at that table, licking cake frosting out of a bowl, or shelling peas and limas, shucking corn, or drying the silverware. When she got older, she sat there with her books and pretend like she was the teacher and you was the student. I knowed she was teaching you to read and write and do figures. I was so proud one of us was gon' be smart as one of them.

"Then her mama died. I don't know how old Miss Ellen was then, but it was the summer you and her used to go sit out behind the barn. Didn't think I knew anything about that, did you? But I did. I reckon I should've done something, but seem like you was the only somebody she wanted to be with. She'd just lost her mother. I think it would have broken her heart if you'd been taken away from her. We was the only family she had." Harriet chuckled. "That chile grew up thinking she was as black as you and me."

Harriet stopped her pretense and looked at Nat, her face stern. "But she ain't black. Sylvie is the black one! You hear me? I don't know what you done to that girl, but she is so mad at you she could eat nails. You ought to apologize to her for whatever you did.

"Now, listen to me. Ellen be back today from Richmond, where she been with Master Gregory's mama getting her wedding dress and the rest of her trousseau. If I know Ellen, she be wanting to see you first thing, especially since her papa ain't here. You hear what I'm saying?"

I nodded. "Yes, ma'am," Nat's voice responded.

"You got to have enough sense for the two of you. You understand what I'm saying?" She smiled and kissed him on the cheek. "I know you do."

And that was how the "conversation" ended. Ekundayo left the kitchen and went to the carpentry shed.

3

Sylvie had known something was wrong the morning after the New Year's Eve party at the big house. Even though Nat had never talked much, even when they were children, she knew when his silence was just silence and when he was hiding behind it. The morning after the party he had been hiding, but now it was the beginning of spring and he was still hiding.

She didn't know why she chose the morning after the party to ask him if he had spoken to Master Chelsea yet about letting him hire out his work like Ezekiel did. She knew he hadn't, because he would have already told her. He would not have kept something that important to her a secret, something that might give them a way out of slavery. Or, if nothing else, at least something to hope for.

Master Chelsea was good that way. He let his slaves make some money, especially ones who had a skill like Ezekiel. When he was caught up with his work for Master Chelsea, he could take his blacksmithing tools into town and to other plantations and earn some cash money. Of course he had to give Master Chelsea part of it, but, still, the rest was Ezekiel's.

Sylvie wanted Nat to earn enough money to buy their

freedom. That would be hard to do, maybe impossible, but just thinking about it made her feel better. She didn't want to end up being a slave all her life like Sister Harriet and get so old she would be too scared to even dream about freedom. Sylvie was dreaming and so were a lot of other slaves. Her brother, George, had told her Gabriel was doing more than dreaming about being free. He was going to do something to get his freedom and he wasn't going to have to pay money to the master to do it.

When Sylvie had asked Nat if he had spoken to Master Chelsea about hiring out, what she really wanted to know was if he was still dreaming about them getting their freedom. She needed to be reassured because she knew he had helped Sister Harriet serve the party and had been around Miss Ellen. When he didn't give her an answer, when he wouldn't even look at her and he put his head down like he didn't want her to see his face, she knew something had happened.

She asked him then if something was the matter. All he said was he didn't know. That was a strange thing to say. Either something was wrong or it wasn't. How could you not know if something was troubling you?

She had never known Nat to be as quiet as he had been since the morning he woke up and a witch had been riding him. Sylvie knew what to do about the witches that came when you were sleeping, but she thought there was another witch riding his spirit and this one had a name. Miss Ellen! When Sister Harriet had told Sylvie the New Year's Eve party was so Master Chelsea could announce that Miss

Ellen was going to marry Master Gregory's son, it was the best news Sylvie could have heard.

How many evenings had she come in from the field when she was a child and seen Nat and Miss Ellen playing outside the kitchen like they were brother and sister? She had been in love with him even then. It didn't matter that she scarcely knew him well enough to speak to since he didn't work in the field. But she saw him every morning when he went to the kitchen with his grandmother. Sylvie liked the way he carried himself, straight up like he knew he was somebody special. On one of those mornings she decided that if neither one of them got sold away, she was going to marry him.

Now she wasn't sure. That morning when she had gone to his cabin and kissed him, he had acted like he didn't know who she was. He had given her this look that said he didn't know why she was kissing him and he wished she would stop. She needed to know, once and for all, how he felt about her, and if he was dreaming about freedom or Miss Ellen.

That afternoon, instead of going back to the slave quarters when she left the field, Sylvie started toward the carpentry shed. She made her way through the tall weeds bordering the field, passed back of the hog pens and the barns, and eventually found herself at the far end of the plantation, where the carpentry shed stood at the end of the row of buildings where Cicero made casks and Ezekiel did his blacksmithing when he was at the plantation.

Sylvie was walking between the last two buildings

when she heard a voice, a woman's voice, coming from the carpentry shed. She stopped. The woman was talking too quietly for her to understand any words, but she recognized that voice, though it had never spoken to her. It was a pretty voice, not rough like hers, and it made Sylvie think of the smell of honeysuckle. The voice was so soft Sylvie imagined that a man could lie on it and go to sleep. She noticed that her teeth were clenched and her hands were balled into fists and her body was so hot that she had begun to perspire.

"He belongs to me," she whispered to herself. "Me! Black Sylvie!" She turned and ran along the side of the building, through the weeds in the back, and into the woods a short distance away. There she fell to the ground beneath a tall pine tree and began crying as memories came back to sting her with the fury of wasps knocked from their nest.

She didn't know how old she was when it happened, but it was the summer she started working in the field. She, George, and their mother, Betty, were leaving the field one afternoon on their way to the quarters when her mother said she wanted to go by the blacksmith's shed and invite Brother Ezekiel for supper. His wife had died a few weeks earlier.

"That po' man ain't got nobody now. His daughter and her baby were sold away around the time you were born, Sylvie, and he liked to have died then. Now Martha up and died, but she been half dead ever since Master Chelsea sold Susannah and the baby away. Anyway, there's only so much aching a body's heart can take. I know you afraid of him because he always look like he's angry. But if any man got a reason to be angry, it's him. Everybody know how come Master Chelsea sold his daughter and her baby. And don't be asking me no questions about it. You too young to be hearing about things like that. But Master Chelsea hates Ezekiel 'cause Ezekiel knows what he did. And now Master Chelsea done something worse. As sick as Martha looked and acted, Master Chelsea kept saying wasn't nothing wrong with her, no matter how much Ezekiel plead with him to send for the doctor. When he finally did send, it was too late. Doctor said if he'd been called sooner, he probably could have saved Martha. That's what Cato heard with his own ears the doctor say to Master Chelsea. Cato say Master Chelsea didn't send for the doctor in time to spite Ezekiel for knowing what he knows.

"Now, to tell the truth, I don't much like Brother Ezekiel myself, but a man whose wife has just died needs to know that folks care about him."

Suddenly, George shouted, "Look, Mama!" and pointed toward the back of the barn.

There sat Nat and Miss Ellen. That was the first time Sylvie remembered feeling an emotion akin to hatred. She didn't understand then what the feeling was or where it had come from. She only knew that she wanted to pull Miss Ellen away from Nat, throw her to the ground, rip her pretty pink dress into pieces, and get her pale white face dirty.

"They holding hands, Mama!" George exclaimed again, louder, knowing there was something wrong with what he was seeing, though no one had ever told him.

Betty shook her head slowly. "I believe I'm going to have a word with Sister Harriet this evening. If Master Chelsea find out his daughter be holding hands with Nat, he'll sell that boy down into Mississippi or Alabama, where they kill niggers just because. Come on, children. I don't want to be nowhere close to them two. Master Chelsea might think I knew about it. Brother Ezekiel gon' have to eat by hisself tonight."

Sylvie never knew what her mother said to Sister Harriet, or if she had said anything at all. Sylvie didn't know if Nat and Miss Ellen continued to sit back of the barn holding hands, because she wouldn't let herself look in that direction when she came from the field. But it was around this time she made a point of being outside her cabin in the morning when Sister Harriet and Nat walked by on their way to the big house. She would say "Good morning," and Sister Harriet would say "Good morning, Sylvie," and Nat wouldn't say anything. Sylvie didn't mind. At least he knew her name now. She started going to Sister Harriet's cabin any evening they came in early from the big house. She would ask Nat if he wanted to do something. He never said no, so Sylvie would take him out in the woods to dig sassafras roots or find skunk cabbage. One time, and she didn't know even now what had come over her, she kissed him on the mouth. He didn't kiss her back but he didn't pull away either. So she kissed him again. In her mind the kissing made them almost like they were married.

Now, however, she wondered what was going on between him and Miss Ellen. Why was she talking to him when she was supposed to be getting married? Maybe the reason Nat couldn't put his arms around Sylvie like she mattered was because Miss Ellen mattered more.

A cold anger came into Sylvie's eyes, replacing the tears. What Miss Ellen was doing wasn't right. There were plenty white men in the world for her. What did she want with Nat? She certainly could not marry him!

Sylvie had to do something, tell someone, but who? Sister Harriet probably knew all about it. And, for that matter, Sylvie's mother probably did, too. Then Sylvie smiled. Gabriel! He probably didn't know his son was fooling with the master's daughter. If anybody would do something, it was Gabriel.

George had been going to the meetings Gabriel had out in the woods late at night, and their mother didn't like it.

"What you want to be listening to Gabriel for?" Sylvie had heard Betty telling George. "I been knowing that little skinny nigger all my life and all I ever heard him talk about is us getting free. Now, don't get me wrong. I ain't in love with slavery, but before I be running away from here, I want to know where I'm going and how I'm going to get there, and Gabriel ain't never give me answers to questions like that."

That was the difference between Sylvie and her mother. Betty needed to know where she was going and how she was going to get there before she would do anything. All Sylvie needed was a dream. Maybe she and Nat weren't dreaming the same dream anymore. Maybe he was dreaming about a somebody he shouldn't be.

She would take care of that.

4

I worked slowly and deliberately as I applied the final coat of finish to the chest of drawers, rubbing the stain in with soft, even strokes. It was late afternoon when I finished, stepped back, and looked at it gleaming like moonshine on a lake. I hoped Nat was pleased.

I was in the back room cleaning my hands with turpentine and a rag when a soft voice came from the doorway:

"Nathaniel?"

The saying of a name by one unmistakable voice. That was all it took. It was as if a key had been inserted into a rusted lock in a heavy door, and the door needed to open only a crack and memories of Ellen came tumbling forth like a spring day that eluded winter's last and desperate grasp. The love and yearning Nat had put into the chest of drawers now flowed from that last scrap of his nyama into mine. Out came not only memories but the passionate exuberance of loving and being loved. However, Nat had never allowed himself to feel these emotions in their full power and instead had put them into the statue at the bottom of the trunk and into the chest of drawers.

Now, for the first time, the love Nat had for Ellen took

full and deep breaths because his body was occupied by a spirit stronger than his would have ever been, a spirit that could withstand the power of the unlived emotions which had sealed Nat into a silent sadness.

I had never known emotions of such intensity, emotions that caused me to feel connected not only to the one who had called Nathaniel forth, but also made me feel joined to everyone, even people I would never know. But I did not want these feelings. I did not like being transformed into a smile so deep that all sorrow was banished. Amma had not sent me to become ensnared by emotion, especially not emotions as intense and consuming as the ones that assailed me at that moment.

Nat's stolid silence had been a bulwark against giving life to Nathaniel, a being created by his love for Ellen and hers for him. But Nathaniel now lived more fully than he ever had, and as I sensed the last shred of Nat's nyama disappearing, I wanted to scream. But even if I had, it would not have mattered. Nat's nyama was no more. His body was truly mine now. My nyama had absorbed all that Nat had been, all Nat had wanted to be, all Nat could have never been in that time and that place.

I was stunned beyond belief. I was no longer just Ekundayo and Nat. Now I was also Nathaniel, and Nathaniel's one purpose in life was to love Ellen.

"Nathaniel?" the soft voice called again.

What I have described occurred in less time than it has taken you to read it, less time even than the pulse of one heartbeat. How quickly and totally one's life can change.

Weak and a little dizzy from the unwanted transformation I had just undergone, I came out of the back room. Standing inside the doorway was a slim young woman in a deep yellow dress with ruffled sleeves. Her hair was long and dark and lay on her shoulders like a silken shawl. Her eyes were the clear, light blue of an early morning when birds competed with each other to see whose song was more beautiful. When she saw me, her thin lips turned up in a smile that matched the one that glowed within my body.

"Ellen," I said softly.

—

She had not seen him since the New Year's Eve party, when her engagement to Gregory had been announced. He was tending the buffet table and it was as if seven years had not elapsed since her father had sent her to finishing school in Nashville and him to work in the carpentry shed. She tried to see him at least once every year during the month she was home from school, but her father did everything he could to prevent that. Sometimes she saw him from the window of her room upstairs when he went to the slave quarters in the late afternoon, and sometimes he would turn and look up as if he knew she was there.

She didn't know what she would have done after her mother died if she had not been able to be with him most of every day. He and Harriet were the only ones who had known how much she hurt, though neither of them ever spoke of it. They knew there were hurts whose pains no words could relieve. Just as they never spoke of her pain at the death of her mother, she never spoke to them about the pain of being slaves.

Many afternoons after dinner, she and Nat had sat behind the barn, or gone to the cemetery and sat beside her mother's grave. On one of those afternoons they became aware of each other as physical beings. Perhaps there had been an innocent brushing of hands, or she had unconsciously touched his arm. Whatever it was, their children's innocence vanished as if it had never had any more substance than early morning dew that evaporated in the warm light of morning. They became awkward with each other, unable to exchange the slightest glance without quickly looking away. She knew, though not in words, that if they looked directly into each other's eyes, there would be no turning back, though there was no way forward either.

Standing there in the doorway now, Nathaniel was looking into her eyes in a way he had never done before; looking at her as if she mattered to him like food and air and water mattered. Ellen felt herself growing warm beneath his gaze, and she smiled nervously before forcing herself to look away. That was when she noticed the chest of drawers on a table at the back of the room.

"It's beautiful!" she exclaimed, going to look closer at it.

"Don't touch it," he warned her. "I just finished putting the last coat of stain on."

Ellen looked closely at the piece of furniture, especially the faces of the drawers. Finally, she turned to look at him, tears in her eyes. "Is this—?" She pointed at the chest of drawers.

Ekundayo nodded. "It's for you."

"Oh, Nathaniel. I–I–don't know what to say. It is so beautiful! Fulani would be so proud of you."

Ekundayo was glad to have something to talk about other than the emotions swirling in him and between them that were begging for release.

"I still miss him," he said. "He was the closest I ever had to a father. He never talked much, and when he did, it was hard to understand him sometimes because of his funny accent. But it wasn't hard to understand him in the way he held a piece of wood, or the way he stroked the grain of a board, or drove a nail straight. I remember the first time I saw him take a stick and carve it into a cane that looked like a snake. Seeing him do that was like watching magic. Fulani wasn't his real name, you know."

"I didn't know. What was it?"

"Guedado. He said it meant 'wanted by nobody.' "

"That's very sad."

"He said that was how he felt."

The words hung in the air. She wondered if that was how Nathaniel felt. How she wanted to tell him that was not so. But perhaps it was better to be wanted by no one than to be wanted and know the wanting could not be satisfied.

They stood side by side, his hand almost brushing against her long yellow dress. He did not dare look at her now, not standing so close. She did not dare look at him either. Instead, they pretended to be looking at the chest of drawers, but only their heads were turned in that direction. Their minds were on each other's presence. She smelled of sunshine and summer grasses and wild roses to him, and he smelled of pine needles and tree bark and rain to her. All she had to do was move her hand the distance of a heartbeat to touch his hand and, like a flame touching paper . . .

Instead, she moved toward the chair in the corner of the room, saying, her voice trembling, "I hated it when my father sent you to work here. He wouldn't tell me where you were and neither would Harriet. It didn't take me long to figure it out, though. And I thought if this was where you were going to be every day, then I would be here, too."

She sat down. He went into the back room, brought out another chair, and placed it next to the table on which the chest of drawers sat. He faced her, but with enough space separating them that he felt safe, from her and himself.

"You used to sit right there in that same chair and you never said a word," he said.

"I would have, if you would have talked to me. But you made like I wasn't even there. I didn't care. I enjoyed watching you and Fulani work. I suppose I was a little jealous, too. We were the same age but you were learning how to make things. I didn't know how to do anything except stitch samplers, and I wasn't very good at that, especially compared to my mother. That was such a horrible year. First, Mama died. Then, Papa wouldn't let you work in the house anymore. He thought that would keep me from seeing you. It didn't, and not long after that I was on my way to Miss Fletcher's Finishing School for Southern Ladies in Nashville."

"I remember the day you left."

"You do?" She was surprised.

"It was raining. My grandmother told me you were leaving that morning. I climbed up in the big oak tree next to the house and waited. I saw you come out of the house and get in the carriage with Master Chelsea. You looked around like you were looking for me."

"I was, Nathaniel. I was."

"I wanted to say something, to do something to let you know where I was, but I was afraid to. I saw the carriage drive off. You turned around and looked back. I watched until the carriage was out of sight."

She smiled. "I tried my best that morning to get away from the house and run down here to tell you goodbye, but Papa wouldn't let me out of his sight for a minute."

"Part of me was sorry you left and part of me wasn't."

She nodded. "I felt the same way."

He hadn't known how to pretend. Alone with her, he was Nathaniel. Then he would have to go back to being Nat, a slave boy training to be a house servant. One afternoon, standing in the corner of the dining room in his blue uniform and white gloves, he remembered that he and Ellen had been talking about her mother the day before. Afraid she would forget her mother, she would tell the same stories about her over and over, and she asked him to tell her everything he remembered. He scarcely remembered anything. The mistress never paid him much attention as long as he did what she told him to. But that afternoon, standing in the corner, he recalled one Christmas when she had told him that he was "a good boy." That had not meant anything to him then and it meant nothing

now, but it might mean a lot to Ellen, and without thinking he said, "Ellen!" Then he saw his white-gloved hands
and remembered this was a time of the day when he was
supposed to be Nat, and he stopped, his mouth open in
consternation. But before he could figure out how to extri-
cate himself from his mistake, Master Chelsea had leaped
from his chair, crossed the room, and slapped him so hard
he was knocked unconscious. It was several days before he
recovered. That was when he learned that Master Chelsea
had wanted to sell him but hadn't. "I told him that if he
sold you, he better sell me, too, because I would die if
he took you away from me," his grandmother told him.
"He said he didn't want you working in the house as long
as Miss Ellen was there. I said fine. It was my idea for you
to go work with Fulani. What Master Chelsea don't understand is keeping you out of the house is not going to keep
Ellen away from you. You be careful. You hear me?"

After that, he could no longer live with the tension of
being Nathaniel some of the time and Nat the rest. He
chose to be Nat all the time and keep Nathaniel hidden,
especially from Ellen. And just as Sister Harriet had said,
Ellen found a way to sneak down to the carpentry shop,
but he would not look at her, though he was glad she was
there. Then Master Chelsea sent her away to school in
Nashville, saying he didn't know anything about raising a
girl. Nat went back to helping Harriet in the mornings and
serving at parties and working in the carpentry shed the
rest of the time.

The years passed. The few times Ellen was able to
sneak to the carpentry shed, she would sit on a chair in the

corner like always and tell him about school and what life was like in Nashville. He seldom said much in return and never let his face show how happy he was to see her. Maybe that was when tiny holes began appearing in Nat's nyama and when its dusky rose color began to fade.

Fulani had known, and last year, only months before he died, he said to Nat, "Love requires a warrior's heart." He had spoken into the silence at the end of the day when they were cleaning their tools and putting them away. It had been as if the old man knew about the sadness in Nat's spirit and what caused it. But when Nat heard Fulani's words, he knew that he did not have the heart of a warrior, and the holes in his nyama grew larger and the vibrant redness changed into a dull brown.

Then came the party that past New Year's Eve. Nat had cleared the buffet table, put out cups, and come in from the kitchen with the large bowl filled with eggnog when Master Chelsea asked everyone to be quiet.

"I have an announcement. It is my esteemed honor and great pleasure to tell you that my lovely daughter, Ellen Amanda Chelsea, is engaged to be married to Gregory Foster IV, the son of my dear friend and neighbor, Gregory Foster III."

Nathaniel looked at her and was startled to see that she was staring at him, sadness in her eyes, and not into the face of her husband-to-be, who was turned toward her, a wide grin on his face. Nathaniel's and Ellen's eyes met for only the slightest of moments, but that was enough. He kept busy filling cups with eggnog, but whenever he glanced in her direction, she was looking at him.

The evening wore on; the eggnog was replaced with champagne. Before too long, most of the guests were inebriated, some more than others. Ellen's husband-to-be had to be assisted to his carriage by his father and the slave coachman. When Master Chelsea passed out and had to be carried upstairs to bed, the few remaining guests departed.

Nat was collecting the dirty cups and glasses from the parlor when Ellen came in.

"Nathaniel," she said softly.

It had been too long since he had heard her call him by that name only she used, too long since he had known himself to be someone other than Nat, a slave. He was surprised when tears sprang to his eyes.

"Oh, thank God!" she exclaimed, seeing his tears. "It has been so long. I didn't know if I still mattered to you, if you remembered."

They sat on the parlor floor before the flaming logs in the fireplace and talked of how big and tall sunflowers had looked when they were children; they talked about sitting behind the barn and watching a hawk sail around and around, high in the sky, and how he had said that was her mother watching over her, and she had never been able to look at a hawk since and not feel safe and protected. He told her how every night when he went to bed he imagined that he was laying his head on her long, dark hair, and how, when he felt more alone than usual, he would imagine her taking his hand in hers and he wasn't alone anymore, and she reached over and took his hand and held it tightly.

"Would you make me something for my wedding?

Something beautiful? Something that I will wake up and see each morning and it will make me think of you? Will you do that for me, Nathaniel? Will you? I have to have you with me in some way. If I don't, I will die being married to Gregory Foster IV."

"Then you won't die," he said. She squeezed his hand and ran from the parlor sobbing.

It was the one moment of his life when Nat was proud of himself.

—

"What are you thinking?" Ellen asked.

"New Year's. Sitting in front of the fire, talking."

"Sitting there with you, I realized that I had missed you more than I had allowed myself to know," she said wistfully.

I sensed Nathaniel wanting to tell her how much he had missed her also, but I could not allow that. "That's not a good thing for a woman to say who is going to be married in a month," I said, somewhat coldly.

I wanted her to go away; I had to be free of the emotions that bound me to her and made me feel so achingly alive. I had a task to perform, a sacred one. The ecstasy of an unexpected love had no place in my life.

She sighed. "Gregory will make a good husband, if a good husband is someone who can give a woman every expensive dress and almost any piece of jewelry she says she wants. I'll be well taken care of, but I'm not a fool. This wedding is not about me and Gregory. It's about the joining of two plantations. Gregory will become the male heir my father never had. He would never think of me, a mere female, as his heir. And he knows; if I were to inherit, I would free the slaves one minute after his body was in the ground.

"Gregory's mother and I had several heart-to-heart talks this past week. She told me all about Gregory's 'friend,' as she referred to her, in Richmond. And if his having a mistress were not bad enough, he also has two children by slave girls. She said the smart wife of a slave owner pretends not to see. Instead, several times a year she makes trips to New Orleans, Charleston, and even New York or Philadelphia, and buys herself whatever her heart desires. And the more mistresses her husband acquires, the more slave babies born who look like him, the more expensive become the things her heart desires.

"What an awful way to live! I want more than that. I want to wake up every morning and be happy that I have another day to be with my husband. I want to sit on the porch with my husband in the evening and be alone with him in the silence." She stopped, then she whispered, "The only person I've ever felt that way about is you."

"Perhaps you've forgotten. I'm a nigger," I said harshly. "The one time I forgot, your father knocked me unconscious. If I forget again, he will kill me."

Ellen looked at me sharply, as if she could not believe what I had said. "That's the first time you've ever said that word around me," she responded. "You know how much I hate it."

"I'm sorry," I apologized. "But I needed to be sure you understood the situation."

"Of course I understand. I thought you knew that. But

things are changing, Nathaniel. Things are going to be different."

"What are you talking about? Is your father going to free us?"

"No. But soon he might not have a choice. Papa's at a meeting in Charleston talking with other slave owners about separating from the United States and starting their own country."

"That doesn't make any sense."

"To them, it does. A man named Abraham Lincoln has just been elected president, and he wants to put an end to slavery. At least, that's what Papa and a lot of the slave owners think. They will go to war to keep slavery. And if the South tries to become its own country, Mr. Lincoln will go to war to keep the country together. No matter how you look at it, there's going to be a war. If Mr. Lincoln wins, you'll be free, Nathaniel. Free! Do you remember when we were children and we would talk about running away to Boston or Canada, somewhere nobody cared what color you were?"

"But we were children then. That was the dream of children."

"I guess I'm still a child then, because I still have that dream, and it's closer to coming true now than ever. Nathaniel, if war comes, there'll be so much confusion. Nobody would notice if you and I disappeared."

"Ellen!" I started to protest.

"Please. Let me finish. I've been thinking about this a lot since New Year's, thinking a lot about how I could be together with the person I really care about and who cares about me. I was hoping war would break out before I had to marry Gregory, but it doesn't look like that's going to happen. So, what to do in the meantime? I thought about us running away, trying to get to Boston, or even Canada. But we would probably be caught and you would be sold down into Mississippi or killed. Then, last month, Papa said he wanted to give me some slaves as a wedding present so I would have my own servants around me. How he could ever think I'd want slaves is beyond me. He said he knew how I felt about slavery, but he would feel better if I had one or two he knew were loyal to me. I started to tell him no, then something occurred to me." She stopped and looked at him, a nervous smile on her face. "What if I asked Papa to give me you?"

"What?" I exclaimed, my voice rising. "You don't honestly think your father would do that, do you?"

"He wouldn't like the idea at first, but because I would be, in his eyes, safely married, he might consider it."

"And if your father gives me to you? Then what?" I asked harshly. "Do you really believe I could live my life pretending to be your slave, calling you 'Miss Ellen' all day, and for what? A few stolen moments alone with you when your husband and his parents weren't around? I couldn't do that, and neither could you."

She was silent, then her confident bravado wilted. "You're right. I'm sorry I brought it up. I knew it was a fantasy, and saying it aloud I sounded like a fool, even to myself."

Just then, I thought I heard something outside, like the sound of someone running. But before I could be sure, Ellen spoke again.

"Nathaniel. You are my passion. I have known you all my life. I don't know what I will do if I can't be with you, if I can't have you."

"You have me," I said simply, turning my head to look at the chest. "My passion, my love is in every inch of that chest. That is all I can do."

Ellen looked at the chest of drawers. "It will have to do, won't it? At least until the war starts." She smiled then and came over to where I was sitting. I stood up. "Nobody in the world calls you Nathaniel except me. That makes you mine. You remember what I told you about your name?"

I smiled. "You said a gnat is an insect. Then you asked me if I was an insect and I said no."

"You're Nathaniel, my Nathaniel." She took my hand and held it, her fingers interlaced with mine. She looked at our hands, first with hers on top, and then mine.

"Our hands look so beautiful together," she whispered.

After a moment she took her hand gently away. She unfastened the cameo brooch pinned over her right breast. "This is so you will have something of me like I will have something of you," she whispered. She put the brooch in my hand and closed my fingers over it. Then she was gone, tears flowing down her face.

I stood there for a long time before opening my hand. It took me a moment to realize that the brooch opened. Inside was a likeness of her. I touched the image lightly with my index finger.

I shut my eyes against the tears that wanted to flow from them, and I tried to will the Nathaniel her presence had evoked back into Nat's nyama. But Nat's nyama no longer existed. Nathaniel's longing was now mine, and I did not like it, or the tears that rolled slowly down my face despite my not wanting them to.

5

Harriet knew more about what went on than even Master Chelsea. The kitchen windows looked out on both sides of the plantation. She never told anyone all she saw. It wasn't nobody's business what folks did as long as no harm was done. She saw the times Dinah eased her way from the field and to the barn where Horace worked. If Master Chelsea had had an overseer, something like that wouldn't have happened, but the last overseer had thought the way to treat slaves was to use a whip on them, until George taught him otherwise. Didn't take Master Chelsea long to realize that somebody who was hurt and angry didn't work as well as somebody who was treated well. So he fired the overseer and put Big Sam in charge of all them what worked in the field. Sam was smart enough to know Dinah would do twice as much work as long as she could spend time in the barn with Horace. Them two really loved each other, but Master Chelsea wouldn't let them marry because Horace wasn't supposed to be no one-woman man. He was like a stud horse and his job was to produce slave babies. Master Chelsea even hired him out to other plantation owners who didn't want to buy slaves if Horace could produce some for them.

Although the field was too far away for Harriet to see anybody's face, she didn't need to. She saw someone's arms moving excitedly and didn't have to see the face to know it was Gabriel. She didn't have to hear him to know he was talking about how God didn't mean for one man to be a slave to another and the day was coming when the Lawd would give him a sign to lead the slaves in a war to win their freedom.

What was the point in talking about being free when you knew it wasn't going to happen? White folks would die before they gave niggers their freedom. She would never understand why Lizzie took up with Gabriel. But the Lawd's ways were not for a poor woman like her to understand. She lost her daughter but she gained the boy. Having him to care for had done a lot to ease the aching in her heart caused by Lizzie's death. At least, that was how it had been until recently.

Something was going on with the boy, but Harriet couldn't put her finger on it. He hadn't seemed like himself lately. She hoped he wasn't brooding over Ellen getting married. Lawd, have mercy! She hoped it wasn't that! That's why she'd had that little talk with him this morning, and not a minute too soon. Ellen had arrived mid-afternoon and had scarcely waited until all her trunks were unloaded off the carriage before she went to see Nat.

Harriet got up from her seat by the window and went to the stove, where she pulled two oblong pans of ginger bread from the oven. She placed the pans atop the stove. Just as she was about to turn back to close the oven door, she thought she saw something out of the corner of her eye. She stopped and looked. It was Ellen coming from the carpentry shed, her head down.

"What you been up to, chile?" Harriet said softly to herself, unsure she wanted to hear whatever this girl she loved like a daughter was coming to tell her.

She was a strange white girl. All through her childhood she preferred sleeping in the cabin with Harriet and Nat and did so as often as her parents let her. She used to work around the kitchen like that was what she was supposed to be doing. One time, her mama came in the kitchen and saw Ellen polishing the silverware.

"I don't understand how a daughter of mine could be white on the outside and nigger on the inside," she had said with disgust, and walked out.

Harriet smiled, remembering how proud Ellen had been to have her mother call her a nigger.

"I'd rather be a slave than own one," Harriet had heard the girl tell her father more than once. "If I was a slave, I'd cut the throat of every white person I saw."

Harriet watched as Ellen started along the path to the kitchen. She was close enough now for Harriet to see the tears on her face.

"Looks like you went and made the aching in your heart worse," Harriet muttered, as she filled a kettle with dippers of water from the barrel in the corner of the kitchen.

Ellen came in, looked at Harriet, and started sobbing. Harriet took the girl in her arms and held her tightly. When Ellen's sobbing began to slow, Harriet led her over to the table and had her sit down. "I got the water on to make us some ginger tea."

Ellen managed a smile. "I'm afraid this is something not even ginger tea can fix, Harriet."

"Maybe not, but ginger tea ain't never made nothing worse."

The two were silent until Harriet brought two cups of tea to the table and sat down across from Ellen.

"What's making your heart hurt so bad?"

Ellen looked up at Harriet. "Why are things the way they are?" she asked, seriously.

"Don't come asking me questions only the Lawd can answer."

"Don't you ever wonder how come you were born colored?"

"Wouldn't do no good if I did. I stays away from wonderings like that."

"I wish I could," Ellen responded plaintively.

"Ain't no point in thinking about what you can't change."

"What if you can't help it? What if the more you try not to think about something, the more you do?"

Harriet took a sip of her tea. "What were you doing down at the carpentry shed?" she asked bluntly.

Ellen lowered her head. "I don't know. It had been so long since I'd seen Nat. And I knew that after the wedding, I might never see him again. I needed to see him one last time."

"And now that you've seen him, you want to see him again."

Ellen nodded. "Seeing him hurt more than not seeing him had."

"What did you expect? What you got to do now is cherish your memories, 'cause that's all you will ever have of Nat."

Ellen shook her head. "No. I'll have the chest of drawers he made for me."

"What chest of drawers?"

"Oh. I thought you knew. It's the most beautiful piece of furniture I've ever seen. When I saw him New Year's, I asked him to make me something for a wedding present."

Harriet didn't say anything but made a noise which Ellen knew was a sign of disapproval.

"Please don't be upset with me for what I'm about to say," Ellen continued. "I had an idea which I proposed to Nat. I realize it was a foolish one, but it sounded fine until I said it out loud."

"What're you talking about?" Harriet asked.

"Well, Papa wants to give me a couple of slaves for a wedding present. I don't want any slaves, but then I thought, what if I asked him to give me Nat?"

Harriet gasped. "Have you lost your mind? Ellen! What's gotten into you?"

"My other idea was for me and Nat to run off together and go to Boston or Canada. I heard that folks up there don't care about who's white and who's colored."

"What did Nat say?"

"He didn't like the idea."

"Thank God, one of y'all still got a little sense."

"What am I supposed to do, Harriet? I can't be with the person I want to be with just because other people don't like his skin color? You tell me what kind of sense that makes. Seems to me that I'm the only one in the whole country who has any sense!"

"Sense is what most folks agree it is."

"You don't believe that, do you?"

"No, I don't, but I got to live by it."

Ellen was silent. She stared at her cup of tea, which she had not touched. Finally, she whispered, "That's not living, Harriet."

"No. It ain't. But it's the best I can do right now."

"So, I'm supposed to marry a man I'll never love and spend the rest of my life pretending that everything is wonderful."

"That's what you'd do if you was a slave," Harriet said bluntly, and then was immediately ashamed. How was it possible that this white girl hated slavery more than she did?

"I suppose I should go," Ellen said, not getting up. "But I need to ask you a question."

"What's that, chile?"

"Is Nat all right?"

"What do you mean?"

"I don't know. He seemed different today. It's nothing I can put my finger on. Just a feeling. Maybe it's that he's grown up. He seemed more like a man today."

Harriet didn't think that's what it was, but all she said was, "Maybe he's got things on his mind."

Ellen stood up. "If one of the things on his mind is going away with me, please tell me."

Harriet was pained by the anguish she saw on Ellen's face. "I don't know if that would be such a good idea, honey."

Ellen nodded as tears came to her eyes again. "You're right," she said softly. "You're right," she repeated, and walked slowly out of the kitchen and along the passageway into the house.

6

You not eating tonight?" I asked Harriet.

From the moment I walked into the kitchen that evening, I noticed that Harriet was distant, almost angry. I assumed it had something to do with Ellen and me.

"Not hungry" was all Harriet said, staring at me from where she stood at the stove.

"I saw Ellen today," I offered, deciding not to wait for her to bring it up.

"What did she want?" the old woman responded gruffly.

I didn't want to tell her because I didn't want to think about Ellen.

"Answer me, boy!" Harriet's angry voice broke into my thoughts. "Don't you be keeping secrets from me. I've known you since the day you were born."

"Ellen wanted to talk."

"About what? Am I going to have to pull the words out of you?"

I saw the anguish on her face and knew I would hate myself if I hurt her. I sighed and said, "She wanted me to run off with her, and since I wouldn't do that, she said she wanted to ask her papa to give me to her for a wedding gift."

"I knew that chile didn't have the sense she was born with. I hope you had enough sense for both of you."

"I did, but she knew we could never be together."

Harriet looked at me intently, as if she was not sure who I was. Finally, she asked me if there was something on my mind. "The last week or so you ain't been like yourself. You upset about Ellen getting married? Is that what's bothering you?"

I looked at her. If anyone had the right to know the truth, it was her.

"I apologize to you, Harriet," I said, but in my own voice.

She recognized not only the change in voice but the change in personality.

"Who are you?" she whispered.

"My name is Ekundayo."

"Where's my boy? Where's Nat? You look like him but you not. Where's my boy?"

"He is here."

"Here where?"

I reached across the table and placed my hand atop hers and squeezed it gently. "Do not be concerned. I have need of his body."

"What are you talking about? What do you mean, you need his body? You some kind of ha'nt? No, that's not it. You must be from Africa."

"Yes. I am."

"I thought so. There's only one person I've ever heard talk like you and that was Fulani. He was an Africa man. He used to tell me stories about how where he come from there were people who could change themselves into gators and snakes and what-in-so-ever. He had a look on his face just like yours, like he knew things we didn't, like he could do things we couldn't. Have you come to take us po' niggers out of slavery?"

I smiled. "Perhaps. I don't know yet. Amma, the chief god of my people, is disturbed because so many blacks have been stolen and so many have been killed, and so many have died. Among my people we believe that every person has an nyama, what you might call a spirit, a soul. When a person dies, his nyama remains in the world. Among my people there are rituals we do so the nyama of the dead will be at peace.

"But things are different since the chalk-faced ones came. They take people and put them on ships and bring them here. So many have died, and their nyama wander over this land like dust blown hither and yon by the wind.

"I am the nyama of a hogon, a spiritual leader of my people. I have been sent to this land to find a way to bring peace to the nyama."

"And I bet you've also come to help us get away from this slavery!" she exclaimed, clapping her hands in glee. "Hallelujah! Thank you, Jesus!"

"I do not know if that is my mission also."

"Trust me, son. That's what the Lawd sent you for.

Now, tell me this. Where is my Nat's en-whatever-you-call-it?"

"Nat's nyama." I did not have the courage to tell her that her grandson was lost to her forever.

"Is it ever going to come back? Am I going to have my Nat back? I don't mean to hurt your feelings or nothing like that, but every Africa man I've ever met has given me the creeps. There was several of them here on the plantation when I was a little girl. My mama said they knew all kinds of things about herbs and roots and which ones to use to cure what and which ones to use to put spells on people. There was this one Africa man; his name was Oba, if I remember rightly. If that man looked at you too hard, you would fall over dead. That's the truth! That was back during the time of Master Ramsey, Miss Charlotte's father. He sold that nigger down to New Orleans, where I hear there's niggers who can out-conjure the devil. You not like that, are you?"

"No, Grandmama," I answered, smiling.

"Good. I don't want to be having to sleep with one eye open."

"I would never harm you."

"I'm happy to hear it. Now, I have one more question for you."

"What's that?"

"What happens to my Nat if you get killed while using his body?"

"Your Nat will be dead."

"Then you better keep yourself from getting killed."

I nodded. "I will do my best."

Harriet shook her head. "Your best ain't good enough. You keep yourself from getting killed. You hear me?"

"Yes, ma'am. I hear you."

7

Gabriel lived alone in a small cabin at the very end of the two facing rows of houses that made up the slave quarters. He had built the cabin and moved into it after Lizzie died giving birth to his son, the son he had never been allowed to hold or even touch. Perhaps it was just as well. He couldn't look at the boy without being reminded of Lizzie. The boy was tall and thin like her and he had the same night-black skin. Seventeen years had passed, and there were nights like this one when her absence hurt even more than it had then. Since they were small, Lizzie had been the only person to whom he could tell anything and everything—his visions, his being chosen by God to be the instrument of His judgment. But Lizzie, like his mother, had died, leaving him all alone.

He had built the cabin away from the others because he didn't want anyone to hear him cursing God for taking the two people who believed in him. And how he had raged and railed against God until one night, emotionally spent after hours of angry prayer, God spoke to him and said, "The Lord thy God is a jealous God. Thou shalt have no other gods before Me." And Gabriel understood. Nothing could stand between him and God, not even feelings of sorrow, not even love of another.

God wanted Gabriel for Himself. That's what his mother had told him on her deathbed. She said the Lawd had come to her in a dream before he was born and told her she was carrying a boy and she was to name him Gabriel after the angel who carried out God's judgment.

He was still a boy when she told him that, but he remembered those words again after Lizzie died. In the little cabin he built next to the woods, Gabriel focused on becoming the instrument of judgment God wanted him to be. He knew what that judgment would be, what that judgment had to be if God was the God of the downtrodden, which Gabriel knew He was. Sometimes God's judgment was merciful and sometimes it was harsh. The one thing it was not was wrong. God could never be wrong.

Gabriel had been having visions since childhood, but hadn't known that's what they were. He thought everybody could look in the sky and see God. Sometimes He looked like a cloud in the shape of a lamb. Other times He stood in the middle of the blue sky with a head like a ram's, a body like a bull's, and eyes shooting streams of fire. Other times God showed Gabriel cities set ablaze with the fire from His eyes, or white people burning in hell, screaming and crying as the fire licked their naked bodies. One time God made it possible for him to read.

He had been in town with his papa, Peter. They were walking in the dusty street next to the raised sidewalk, where only white people were allowed to walk. Just as they were going past a store, Gabriel looked up and saw the writing on the window. Always before he had seen writing as nothing more than lines going in different directions. This time, however, he saw that the lines were letters and the letters made words and he said, "General Store, Papa."

"What you talking about, boy?"

Gabriel pointed at the store window. "That's what the words say."

A few days later, Peter stole a Bible from a little church he and some other slaves were painting, and gave it to Gabriel, who read from it every night to his parents. But nobody except Lizzie knew that God walked and talked with him until that Sunday when the leaves had changed colors and were falling from the trees. The slaves were gathered in Master Chelsea's front yard pretending to listen to Reverend Thorndyke.

He didn't know what year that happened, but he was twelve, the same age as Jesus when he preached in the temple. It was the Sunday every month when the white preacher from town came out to preach to the slaves. Reverend Thorndyke was a bald-headed, roundish white man with a face so red folks were afraid he was going to fall over dead. Which is what happened the next summer. He was standing on the sidewalk outside the general store. It was so hot that the shade underneath the trees went looking for shade. Reverend Thorndyke was mopping the sweat off his brow and head with a big red handkerchief and he sighed once and fell to the ground. Gabriel had been in town that day with his father and saw what happened. It looked like the Lord had been holding Reverend Thorndyke up by a string attached to the top of his head and got tired of holding it, or maybe He got distracted by some evil the white folks were doing and forgot about Reverend Thorndyke and let the string slip through His fingers.

The white man hadn't been much of a preacher. Every month he said the same stuff about God not liking disobedience and how God meant for niggers to be slaves because Ham looked at Noah when Noah was naked. Gabriel didn't understand why he deserved to be a slave because Ham saw his papa naked. He knew that Reverend Thorndyke didn't know either. The white preacher didn't know anything about God, not like Gabriel did.

That autumn Sunday morning Gabriel was sitting on the grass with Lizzie, Sister Harriet, and his parents. He wasn't listening to Reverend Thorndyke. Instead he was looking at the sweat pouring off the white man's head. All of a sudden the sweat turned into tiny wriggling snakes. Gabriel jumped up, his body twitching like a fish on a hook.

"Sinner! Sinner!" he shouted, pointing at Reverend Thorndyke. "I see the snakes! I see the snakes coming out of your head and crawling down your face. The snake that caused Adam and Eve to sin against the Lord Almighty, the snake that tempted Eve with the fruit, the snake that damned you and me." His eyes rolled back into his head until only the whites were showing. "Lord! Come down this morning and help this po' sinner man, this man who has never believed in You, this man who does not know You, this man who has not seen Your fiercesome face."

Reverend Thorndyke burst into tears and sank to his

knees, sobbing, saying over and over, "Jesus! Jesus! Can you forgive me for being a fraud? Please forgive me, Jesus!"

Gabriel ran to the Reverend, put his hand on the white man's head, looked into the sky where he saw God just as plain as the others saw only a blue sky. That morning God was a yellow beam encircling the sky and Gabriel smiled when he saw it.

"Hallelujah! Hallelujah!" he shouted. "Praise God! The Lord forgives you, Reverend. He says you are to go in peace."

Reverend Thorndyke wrapped Gabriel in his flabby arms and hugged him to his chest so tightly Gabriel could hardly breathe. "Thank you, brother! Thank you! I've been saved. Yes, Lord! I've been saved!"

And with those words he got on his mule and rode back to town.

Master Chelsea never hired another white preacher. Gabriel knew more about God than any preacher Master Chelsea had ever heard. Every Sunday after that, Gabriel had preached to the slaves in the quarters and told them stories about how God had freed the Israelites from the Egyptians, and how Moses led the people through the Red Sea without anybody getting so much as a drop of water on him. He told them about Samson using his strength to bring down the building on his enemies, about Shadrach, Meshach, and Abednego being thrown in the fiery furnace and walking out without a hair on their heads being singed, about Daniel in the lion's den and how God had made the lions lie down and purr like kittens.

Sometimes Master Chelsea and the mistress came to

hear Gabriel preach. They didn't seem to mind that Gabriel wasn't telling the slaves to obey their masters and mistresses and love white folks. Instead they enjoyed the singing, even when Gabriel led the slaves in singing:

Didn't my Lord deliver Daniel, Daniel, Daniel.
Didn't my Lord deliver Daniel,
Then why not every man?

After services Master Chelsea would pat Gabriel on the back and tell him he was a better preacher than any white man he'd ever heard.

Gabriel wondered if Master Chelsea really understood that he was telling the slaves that God wanted them to throw off their bondage and He would help them. On any other plantation, Gabriel would have been whipped and probably sold away if the slave owner heard him telling the slaves things like that, but Master Chelsea didn't seem to care. It took Gabriel a while before he figured out how smart Master Chelsea was. A slave owner who beat his slaves was unintentionally teaching them to hate slavery and white folks. But a slave owner like Master Chelsea, who let his slaves have their own gardens and sell vegetables in town, who let those with skills hire out their time and live away from the plantation, who let one of his slaves preach rebellion, a slave owner such as that was teaching his slaves that slavery wasn't bad, that slavery didn't hurt, that slavery could feel like freedom! A slave owner that smart was worse than one who beat his slaves.

Gabriel got out of bed. Sleep was ignoring him as it

had done for more nights than he could remember. He went to the door, opened it, and looked up into the night sky. It had been on a night like this just last week when he had looked up and seen, spread against the night sky, the ram-headed God holding a long sword made of fire. Arrayed against the Almighty were white people almost as numerous as the stars. But that didn't stop God. He raised that flaming sword and the sword grew longer and longer until it stretched from God's hands to the farthest point of the universe. Then God swung it and killed all the white people in the world.

He had always known this would be God's judgment, and Gabriel was ready to carry it out, but he needed one more man. He would not go to war without the same number Jesus had when he waged war against the unrighteous. God would not allow His judgment to be carried out if he did not have twelve men who knew that whites were born of the Devil and could not do good no matter how hard they tried. The white man's nature was evil from the moment he was conceived and it became more evil with every breath he took, from the first one to the last. And the white woman! Gabriel shuddered at the thought of the depth and breadth of her evil. He had seen them in town, seen them when they came to the plantation for the parties that Master Chelsea's wife put on when she was alive. He had seen them in their long gowns and hair in curls, each one of them more wicked than Jezebel.

He remembered his brother, Enos, who died in the fall of the same year God showed Gabriel how to read. A few years older than Gabriel, Enos had been picking grapes from vines near the road that went past the plantation. A carriage came along driven by a slave. Inside was a white man and his daughter. The man saw Enos picking grapes and told the slave to stop. The man called out to Enos and asked him to bring him a big bunch of grapes. Enos came running up to the carriage to give the man the grapes. The man took the grapes and drove off without giving Enos so much as a penny. But later that day, the man's daughter told her papa that Enos had looked at her and made a face like he had put a curse on her. Rose, Gabriel's mama, said Enos had more sense than that, that he knew what happened to a nigger who looked at a white woman.

What Enos had to say didn't matter against the word of a white woman. Gabriel remembered the night the white men came to the cabin and took Enos, saying he had to pay the price for what he had done. Sometimes Gabriel could still hear his mother and father screaming and crying as the white men dragged Enos away. They hung him from a big oak tree by the side of the road just outside of town and left his body hanging there for the crows and the buzzards to peck at.

Gabriel's mama died not too long after that and his father might as well have. Peter seemed to forget that he still had a son. Or maybe he remembered, but that son didn't matter as much as the dead one. At least that was how Gabriel saw it. He would read to his father from the Bible, but Peter didn't seem to hear. Nothing Gabriel said brought comfort to the sorrow in Peter's soul. He retreated more and more into silence and eventually died. Gabriel didn't remember when, and he had not gone to the burying. As far as he was concerned, his father had died a long time ago and his body had just needed time to catch up.

That white man's daughter had killed three people with her lie, had killed people she had never laid eyes on. When a white man wanted to kill a nigger, he had to use a gun. A white woman was more powerful than that. All she had to do was whisper, "That nigger looked at me," and that nigger was as good as dead.

Gabriel had to do something before his own son was dead from a white woman's word. He kept thinking about what Sylvie had told him a few evenings ago. He didn't want to believe it, but Sylvie had put her hand on the Bible and sworn that she had heard Nat and Master Chelsea's daughter talking about how much they loved each other. Before he could start handing out justice to white people, he had to save his own son before a white girl's evil tongue got him killed just as it had Enos.

——

"Afternoon, son."

I turned and saw a short, thin man walking through the doorway of the carpentry shed. The man was smiling, but it was not the kind of smile that would evoke an answering one. Perhaps it was the spaces between the man's teeth which gave the smile more of an evil cast than he might have intended. But then there were the eyes, dark and so intense it seemed that they could make flames leap from wet logs.

I recognized that this was Nat's father, and I returned his greeting without emotion.

Gabriel came in slowly, looking at me intently. Then he shook his head.

"I'm glad you took after your mama when it comes to looks. You got the same pretty black skin and sad eyes." He smiled. "Aren't you glad to see me, boy?" He laughed dryly. "Don't answer that. It might not be something I want to hear. How could you be glad to see your father after listening all your life to what Sister Harriet had to say about me. That ol' woman threatened to have Master Chelsea sell me down into Alabama or Mississippi if I came near you. You didn't know that, did you?"

I shook my head, although I did know it.

"What's the matter, son? Cat got your tongue? Your papa comes to pay you a visit and you don't know what to say?"

It was true. I didn't know what to say. This man, "my father," had a way about him unlike that of any slave I'd met. Where the eyes of other slaves were dull with shame, Gabriel's eyes gleamed with a ferocity I envied. Here was a man who had no doubts, no uncertainties.

Gabriel walked to the far end of the room and looked at the chest of drawers. "Did you make this?"

I nodded.

Gabriel shook his head in admiration. "That's some mighty fine work. If you were a white man, you could make a good piece of money turning out furniture like this."

Gabriel sat down in the chair, the same one Ellen had sat in. I sat on the end of the worktable.

"Ol' Fulani couldn't have done as good a job as you did on that chest of drawers," Gabriel continued. "Who did you make that for?"

"Master Chelsea's daughter. She's getting married."

"She is gon' be lucky to have a piece of furniture like that. Just like the white folks is lucky to have a nigger like you, a nigger who can do anything with wood. God blessed you, son. Gave you the ability to take wood and create something beautiful. Now, answer me this: How you think God feel about you using that ability he gave you to make furniture for white folks? Huh? How you think God feel about that? Don't you think God gave you that ability for you to use for yourself and your people? I expect Sylvie would love to have a chest of drawers that pretty. What do you think?"

"I reckon she would," I said finally.

Gabriel gave a dry laugh. "You reckon. Don't you know?" he asked, his voice suddenly getting louder. "I know damn well she would! But you probably don't think a nigger woman deserves a chest of drawers as pretty as that. What would black Sylvie do with something like that? She ain't got no clothes to put in it. All she's got is a couple of dingy dresses. What she gon' do with a chest as pretty as that? Maybe if she had a chest like that, with all them pretty carvings on the drawers, well, maybe she'd feel like there was somebody what cared about her." Gabriel stopped. The ends of his lips turned up in what I presumed was meant to be a smile but looked more like a grimace. "Don't feel bad, son. It ain't your fault. Sister Harriet raised you, and she raised you to love the white folks. If

Master Chelsea was to fart in her face, she'd grin and say, 'Sho do smell good, massa. Please fart some more.' " Gabriel laughed. "But you ain't gon' be like that. I come down here to save you from the white folks and make a man out of you.

"There's a war coming, son. White folks think us'n don't know what's going on. Well, I know! Somebody named Lincoln been elected president and the slave owners are as mad as mad can be. They say Lincoln gon' get rid of slavery. Slave owners say he'll do it over their dead bodies. I don't know which white folks to believe and I ain't waiting to find out. If we wait on the white folks to make up their mind to free us, we'll be slaves as long as we black. We got to free ourselves. You hear me, son? We gon' free ourselves and it's gon' be soon, too."

Gabriel got up and came and put an arm around my shoulder. "I want you, my son, my flesh and blood, I want you next to me when we strike our blow for freedom. Will you stand with me, son?"

I knew how Nat would have responded and said, in Nat's voice, "Sister Harriet say you dangerous. She say I should stay away from you."

Gabriel raised his eyebrows. "Me? Dangerous? Truth ain't dangerous. I think the world of your grandmother, despite how she kept me away from my own son. Sister Harriet is as good a soul as there is on this plantation, but she done spent more of her life with the white folks than she has us niggers. She know what Massa Chelsea gon' say before he do. She believe that we was born to serve the white folks, but that ain't what the Bible say.

"The Bible say that God delivered Daniel from the lion's den and the Hebrew children from the grasp of the Egyptians. The Bible talks about Joshua and how God brought down the walls of Jericho when Joshua blew on his horn. The Bible tells me that God is on our side, that God is waiting for us to strike the first blow and He'll do the rest.

"There's gon' be a meeting tonight, son. I want you to come. I need you there. Listen for an owl to hoot three times. That'll be the signal. You won't have to wonder about which way to go. Just follow the others. Am I gon' see you tonight?"

"Maybe," I said.

"I'll take that for a yes." Gabriel chuckled and then left.

For a long while after he was gone, I scarcely moved. Too much was happening too fast. As long as my nyama had merely occupied Nat's body, my purpose had been clear. Find the way to bring peace to the nyama of the dead. But my nyama was not the same anymore. Instead of me using Nat's body and nyama, Nat had used mine to bring Nathaniel into existence. And Nathaniel cared passionately about life and love, and he had listened eagerly to Gabriel's words of rebellion and freedom. Nathaniel knew nothing of nyama and their needs. He wanted happiness for himself. I did not understand such selfishness because my desire could not be separate from Amma's desire.

Then it occurred to me: what if the nyama could not find peace until they had avenged themselves on the Soul Stealers? Amina's father had called the nyama into battle when the Soul Stealers came to his village. I did not know what words he had used to command the nyama. But perhaps I did not need to. The nyama who came in the holds of the slave ships and those created by the cruelty of the Soul Stealers on plantations were probably thirsting for justice. If they saw Gabriel and his followers going into battle against the Soul Stealers, maybe they would seize the opportunity to balance the scales and satisfy their own need.

I did not see that I had anything to lose by going to Gabriel's meeting.

8

Whoo! Whoo! Whoo!

The sound came from just outside the cabin. I was already awake, not having slept much for fear I would not hear the signal. At the same time, I would not have been sorry had I slept through it. I was afraid of what I might be getting myself into. But at the same time, I was excited to be doing something to strike a blow against slavery. That was what I was now—a slave. Even if I discovered the way to care for the nyama, I would still be a slave. I refused to live my entire life as another man's property.

Whoo! Whoo! Whoo!

I rolled quickly and quietly out of bed.

"Where you goin', son?" Harriet asked from the other side of the room.

I had hoped she wouldn't hear me, but I was not surprised she did. "Gabriel's having a meeting."

"What you want to go to that for? He don't mean nobody good, colored or white."

I didn't want to believe that. Gabriel was the first black man I'd met who hated being a slave so much that he was willing to do something about it. Harriet was old, and though she might not have loved being a slave, she didn't hate being one either. "I need to see for myself."

"My word ain't good enough for you?" she asked, as if what I was about to do was an insult to her.

"You said yourself that maybe I was sent here for more than to bring peace to the nyama. Maybe you're right. Maybe I have been sent here to help free the slaves. Maybe the nyama will not know peace until the slaves are free. Knowing what I must do has not told me how to do it. Maybe Gabriel's way is the first step toward accomplishing what Amma sent me to do."

"If you think the foolishness Gabriel talks is goin' to help us niggers get free, I don't want to have nothing to do with you. You might look like my Nat, but Nat wouldn't do this to me."

I wanted to tell her that this wasn't about her. Instead, I said nothing and went out the door.

Whoo! Whoo! Whoo!

The sound of the "owl" came from the woods at the edge of the slave quarters. I stood for a moment until my eyes adjusted to the darkness. Then I saw other figures moving quietly in that direction and followed them.

Whoo! Whoo! Whoo!

When I reached the trees, there was a path leading into them and, ahead of me, a man moving confidently forward. I followed him, and before long I entered a clearing. A small fire at the center illuminated Gabriel standing next to it, arms folded across his chest.

Men were seated on the ground in a semicircle around

him. I sat down at the end farthest from Gabriel and looked around. Sylvie's brother, George, was there, as was Little Sam, son of Big Sam, the overseer. I was surprised to see Cato. He was the son of Charlotte Chelsea's father, Octavius Ramsey, who had refused to recognize him. He had kept his bitterness hidden behind jokes and grins. Whenever there was a party at the big house, Master Ramsey, and now Master Chelsea, had Cato come to tell stories to entertain the white people. I wondered if Master Chelsea would believe that Cato looked as if he went to sleep every night fantasizing about putting a knife through the heart of a white person, any white person. Because he was the oldest man there, it was as if he had the most time to cultivate his hatred. Sitting next to him was Ezekiel, his face a dark mask of fury. Even though the blacksmith shed was next to mine, this was the first time I'd seen Ezekiel. I supposed he was working on another plantation.

"My brothers!" Gabriel said, breaking the silence. "Welcome! Welcome! I especially want to welcome someone new. My son, Brother Nat!" He pointed to me. "Now that he has joined us, we number twelve, not counting me."

"Brother Gabriel!" It was Ezekiel. He stood up.

"What's on your mind, my brother?" Gabriel asked.

"I don't mean no disrespect, and I know this boy over here is your boy. But I know this boy, too, and to my mind, he ain't nothing but a house nigger. How do we know that Master Chelsea won't hear everything we say tonight by sunup? Anybody else agree with me?"

Every hand went up except mine and Gabriel's.

Gabriel looked around the semicircle, his eyes pausing on each man, a sneer on his face. "Sit down, Ezekiel," he commanded.

The blacksmith hesitated. "You been saying for some time that we needed a twelfth man. I think you forgetting that Jesus's twelfth man was Judas and he was the one who betrayed Jesus."

"I said sit down!" Gabriel roared.

Ezekiel slowly sat back down on the log.

"If any of you knew anything, you'd know that an army has only one general. That's right! One general! And all decisions are made by that one general. I am the general of this army! I decide who's in the army and who's out. That boy there is my flesh and blood, and if I say he's in, he's in! Is that clear? Brother Ezekiel? Is that clear?"

Ezekiel stared back at Gabriel.

"Is that clear, Brother Ezekiel?"

Reluctantly, Ezekiel nodded.

"Is that clear?" Gabriel asked again, looking at all the men.

"Yes," a few muttered.

Even though Gabriel coerced the others into agreement, it was clear to me that my presence was not only not wanted but that I was already thought of as a traitor. I wanted to get up and leave, but I could see how much my being there meant to Gabriel. And if I left, I would always wonder if whatever Gabriel was planning would have led to what I was supposed to do to take care of the nyama. So, despite my discomfort, I stayed.

"As I was saying," Gabriel began again, "there are now

twelve of you, the number of disciples Jesus had. And just as the Lawd sent Jesus into the world to redeem sinners and punish the unrighteous, the Lawd has sent me here to redeem my people from slavery. Do you understand what I am saying? With the help of the twelve of you and the Lawd's mighty arm, we will free our people from the white man's cruelty and make the white man pay for his sins.

"There are great changes coming, my brothers. God Almighty is preparing to move against these evil white people. They think we don't know what's going on in the world. They think all we know is what takes place here on the plantation. But they're wrong.

"Master Chelsea lets Brother Ezekiel go to other plantations and into town to work. The white folks think Brother Ezekiel is as dumb as the horses he makes shoes for, so they talk like he can't hear and think as good as they can. But Brother Ezekiel has good ears and a good mind, and when he comes back here, he tells me what he learned.

"Brother Ezekiel say that the white folks can't talk about nothing but a man named Lincoln. Seems that this man, this Abraham Lincoln, is the new president of the United States, and he say he going to put an end to slavery. The white folks don't like that kind of talk and they say they going to start their own country, that they going to separate themselves, and the United States won't be united any longer.

"There was another white man. His name was John Brown and he didn't wait for nobody to end slavery. He got himself together an army made up of black and white and he went around killing white folks and freeing black.

The white folks couldn't have that, so they caught ol' John Brown and hung him.

"Now, I'm pleased, mighty pleased, to hear about Mr. Lincoln and Mr. Brown, but I'm not going to sit here and wait for some white men to give me my freedom. No, sir! I'm going to take my freedom for myself!"

"Amen!"

"Tell the truth, Gabriel!"

"That's right!"

"For all we know, Mr. Lincoln might never get around to freeing us niggers on the Chelsea plantation. Some white folks might kill him like they done John Brown. We can't depend on white folks that don't even know we exist. We can't depend on nobody but ourselves. You understand me?"

"We hear you!"

"The time has come for us to fight for freedom! I had a vision, brothers. Oh, yes! I had a vision. I saw a mighty army of black men spread across the heavens. They were armed with shovels and hoes and pitchforks, but they weren't marching to the fields to make crops for the white folks. Oh, no! Because on the other side of the heavens was an army of white men, and these white men had guns and knives and swords. But they didn't have the greatest weapon of all. *That* weapon was with the black men. And you know what that weapon was, my brothers? It was God Almighty Himself! I saw the Lawd, and His head was like that of a lion, and fire came from His nostrils. He had the body of a man but there were great wings growing out of His back. He walked on two legs but His feet were horses' hooves. In His hands He held bolts of lightning. He turned and looked at me and He said, 'Gabriel? Gabriel? Do you not know that it is better to die trying to be free than to live as a slave?' And I answered, 'Lawd, I know!' And He asked, 'What do you know, Gabriel?' And I said, 'Lawd, I know it is better to be dead than to be a slave!' And the Lawd looked at me and said, 'My son! My son!'

"And then the black men on one side of heaven charged the white men on the other side of heaven and the battle began. You should have seen the blood! You should have seen the blood! Rivers of blood flowing from the bodies of white men and black men, but while the white men groaned and cried as they died, the black men laughed and shouted. The black men knew. Death in the cause of freedom gives life to a man, while life as the white man's slave is the worst kind of death. The blood of white men flowed over me and washed me clean of all doubt, of all questions, and I heard the voice of God call out: 'Gabriel! Gabriel! Will you join the army of God?' And I said, 'Yes, Lawd! Yes! You lead, and I will march behind you wheresoever you lead me. Even unto death!' "

Gabriel paused and looked at each face in the semicircle of men. "Can you kill a white man?" he asked in a whisper. "Would you rather die than live as a slave?"

He came to the first man. "Brother Frederick! Stand up! Look into my eyes and answer me. Can you kill a white man?"

"Show him to me and he's a dead man!"

"Would you rather die than live as a slave?"

"Yes!"

Gabriel embraced the man and then turned his cold stare on the next one.

I listened to Gabriel's words. They sounded true and good, but something was wrong because I didn't feel that he was telling us the whole truth. I looked around the semicircle at everyone sitting, standing up only to embrace Gabriel as he asked each the same two questions. Then I knew what was bothering me.

Among my people, when there was an important matter to be decided, all the men gathered in the toguna. It was an unusual-looking structure, open on all sides with the roof so low that a man could not stand to his full height. If, during discussions, someone in his excitement stood up to speak, he would hit his head against the logs and thatch of the ceiling. The blow would make him stop talking, remember himself, and control his emotions. My people believed that true words could be spoken only when a man was sitting. This was called good speech. Speech made while a man was standing smelled of death and was evil.

That was when I smelled the thick, pungent odor coming from Gabriel. He stank worse than cow manure rotting in the sun. He did not care about freeing the slaves. He was saying what he knew the others wanted to hear. But whatever he was planning was going to end with all of us dead.

I waited nervously now as Gabriel moved closer and closer to where I sat. There was a malevolent grin on his face as he asked, "Can you kill a white man?" Each one answered as if he would enjoy killing a white man. I did not understand. In one of the visions Time had shown me, I had seen Soul Stealers deriving pleasure from murdering for no other reason than they had the power and means to do so. Were Gabriel and the other eleven no better than Soul Stealers?

I was sick to my stomach when I realized what a terrible mistake I had made by coming. But it was too late to do anything about it. If I did not answer yes to Gabriel's questions, would Gabriel kill me? Probably not with his own hands, but I had no doubt that Brother Ezekiel would do it gladly.

Gabriel was standing before me now, his grin more demonic than ever. I stood up to face him.

"My son! Can you kill a white man?"

"Yes," I forced myself to say.

"Would you rather die than live as a slave?"

"Yes," I repeated, hoping I sounded convincing. I knew I hadn't when the grin vanished from Gabriel's face and eyes and was replaced by compressed lips and a hard stare. I waited nervously, afraid of what he was going to do. We stared at each other for a moment, and I saw a look of contempt for me come into Gabriel's eyes. He turned away and returned to his place beside the small fire.

Gabriel took a large knife from the waist of his pants. Holding up his left hand so we could see, he made a long cut in the palm, without flinching or wincing. Instead, he grinned.

"Come. Each of you. Drink my blood. My blood will bind us, each to the other and each to death."

One by one the men walked forward and pressed their

lips to Gabriel's bleeding palm. I stood at the end of the line and I looked into the face of each man as he walked past me to return to his place. Their teeth and lips were stained blood-bright-red and the ends of their mouths were turned upward in twisted smiles.

What were they feeling? How could the thought of killing and dying make them happy? Didn't they know that all whites were not evil? What if they killed a man like Josiah, or a woman like Ellen? You couldn't know who was good and who was evil by the color of his skin. Didn't they know that?

The line reached its end and there I stood, looking at Gabriel's palm. The blood in it had been mixed with the saliva of the eleven men who had already put their mouths to that palm. I hesitated, then closed my eyes as my lips barely touched Gabriel's palm.

As I turned to move away, Gabriel grabbed me by the back of my neck and shoved his bloody, spit-wet palm into my face. I gasped and tried to pull away, but Gabriel was strong and his grasp firm, and he rubbed his palm all over my face, smearing it with blood and spit.

"You belong to me now," Gabriel whispered in a strangled voice. "You understand me, boy? If you even think about saying anything to that ol' lady who brought you up, or to Master Chelsea, I will let Ezekiel kill you, which he would love to do. You understand me?"

I nodded. "Yes," I said in a weak voice. Gabriel released his grip on my neck and pushed me away. I stumbled back to my place at the end of the semicircle.

Gabriel raised his cut palm and put his lips to the cut and sucked at it loudly. When he raised his head, his teeth were bright red.

"Now we belong to each other, and each of you now belong to me. The next time you hear the owl hoot three times will be the time we will go out to do the Lawd's work. Be strong, my brothers! Be strong!"

He took a handful of dirt and put it on the fire. The flames sputtered for a moment and then died away. The men moved into the darkness and onto the path back to the plantation.

I followed, but at a distance. With the blood and spit covering my face, I felt dirty to the very depths of my being. The men I was following moved fast, and without someone to follow I was quickly lost. I found myself stumbling into the woods. Low-hanging branches lashed at my face as I stumbled into trees so big around they seemed to have been growing since Amma created the world. I don't know how long I wandered in the woods, but finally I came to a large and still lake. I ran to it and, instead of just washing my face, I dove into the water. I needed every part of me cleansed.

The water was so cold it almost took my breath away, but I swam deeper down beneath the water's surface. I needed to be clean again and thought I would not be until I touched the lake's bottom. I kept swimming deeper and deeper. There didn't seem to be a bottom. My chest began to tighten and I propelled myself upward, gasping loudly when I broke the surface, my breath ragged. I swam to the shore and dragged myself out of the water.

I was shivering from the cold that was so intense it made my skin burn. Eventually, my shivering ceased. Through the thick foliage on the trees, I could see faint patches of bright blue. Another day had begun. In the faint light that managed to make its way into the forest, I noticed a great bird, with night-black feathers, perched high on a limb on the other side of the lake.

"What have I done?" I whispered aloud to the bird. "What have I done?"

The bird did not respond.

9

In the days that followed, I stayed busy. I didn't want to think about the next time the "owl" called and what was to happen. So I found boards on the horse stalls in the barn that needed replacing, as did ones on the pigsties and the corncribs. The posts in the fences surrounding the chicken yard could use a little shoring up. And I made a couple of coffins because it was good to have some on hand for the unexpected inevitable. But I stayed away from the carpentry shed as much as possible in case Ellen decided to visit again. I did not want to see her, did not want her to say that name and call me into intimacy.

On the day she was married, Master Chelsea called all the slaves to the front of the house to tell "Miss Ellen" goodbye and sing a song to her as she left for the church in Richmond where the wedding was to be. But I went into the woods and looked for trees that could be cut down and taken to the sawmill and cut for lumber.

Harriet had scarcely spoken to me since the night I went to Gabriel's meeting, not even in that indirect way when she seemed to be mumbling to herself. I missed that, missed her, missed her caring about me. But how could she? I had not only taken her grandson from her; I had done something her grandson would not have. I could not imagine how difficult, how painful it must be for her to look at me and see Nat but know that the person inside was someone else. I dreaded the day I would have to tell her Nat no longer existed.

I stayed away from everyone as much as I could, especially those who had been in that semicircle. But as I moved around the plantation with my tools, I could not avoid seeing some of them—Cato, George, Ezekiel, and others. They eyed me with suspicion. I wanted to ask them: "Is it slavery you hate, or just white people?" But as I thought about it, I wondered: could you hate one without hating the other? White people made it easy to hate them by the evil they did. However, you couldn't tell which ones were evil and which were not by looking at them. So it was easier to say they were all evil. But how was that different than them thinking all of us were ignorant savages? Slave and slave owner judged, with ultimate harshness, everyone of the other race, without truly knowing anyone.

I did not want to be part of that, but if I voiced my questions and concerns aloud, Ezekiel would have his excuse to kill me. I had no choice; I was going to be involved in a bloodletting. My only hope was that the nyama would come and fight alongside us. If they did, I would know they approved of Gabriel, that they needed their revenge before they could have peace. And I would also know that words spoken while standing *could* be true.

But could the nyama come on their own? I probed deeply into my vast memory for the words to the song Menyu and Amina's father sang that had brought forth nyama to kill the Soul Stealers. The words should have been part of my memory. If the words were part of my memory something or someone was keeping them hidden from me.

But even if the words were revealed to me, how many of the nyama here would have understood them? None. The words were useless in this place. If the nyama were going to come and help destroy slavery, they would do so without assistance from me.

Slavery was a kind of chaos, a confusion of mind which distorted everyone's vision by making skin color an object of worship. Maybe killing white people was the only way the rightful order could be restored.

Maybe, I tried to convince myself.

—

Whoo! Whoo! Whoo!

I was not asleep. The time had come. I was terrified. Perhaps I was supposed to be. A man should not go out to kill without trembling. However, part of my fear was that I was the only one of the thirteen afraid to kill.

I would have felt somewhat better if Amma had given me a dream or some sign that the nyama would come today. Maybe he was testing me to see if I had the resolve to do what needed to be done. Perhaps the nyama in this land could only know peace when white people knew the same pain blacks did. For that to happen, would whites have to see *their* loved ones lying dead at black hands?

I got up and looked across the room to where Harriet lay. I couldn't see her in the dark, but I doubted that she was asleep. She had heard the "owl," too. I wanted to say something to her. Not knowing what, I left.

I was the last one to arrive at the clearing in the forest. Some of the men were carrying shovels; others had pitchforks. Still others had swords and knives which looked as if they had been fashioned by Ezekiel in the forge. I was empty-handed.

I saw Gabriel and George a short distance away. George's hands were moving rapidly and it was clear he was angry about something. Gabriel suddenly turned his back on George and walked away, even though George was still talking. It was obvious that Gabriel didn't want to listen to George anymore.

"My brothers!" Gabriel called out, his voice trembling with excitement, a rusty sword in his hand. The men gathered before him in a semicircle. "My brothers! The time has come! Before we go, let us bow our heads in prayer."

Everyone, except me, lowered their heads and closed their eyes.

"Lawd, this is your servant, Gabriel, talking to You from the pit of night."

"Yes," several men sang quietly.

"Lawd, You have talked with me since I was a child. And Your words have always been the same: 'Gabriel. Go and free my people.' "

"Amen!"

"Yes, Jesus!"

"Lawd! Like You came to Moses and told him to free the Hebrew children, so You came to me! You have shown me visions of a war when black will go against white, and in that vision, You have let me see You in all Your glory and majesty, standing on the side of the slave, on the side of us poor black people who don't have anyone but You to depend on."

"Have mercy!"

"This morning, Lawd, we are going out to do Your work!"

"Yes, Jesus! Yes!"

"We are going out to show these evil white people that God don't like ugly!"

"No, he don't!"

"God don't like seeing His people with their heads bloodied. God don't like seeing His people crying way up into the night 'cause their husbands, wives, and chillen been sold away from them. God don't like a world where evil has the upper hand. We go this morning, Lawd, to bring Your goodness to this land. But to do that, we are going to have to shed the blood of our enemies and Your enemies, God. The blood is going to have to flow like a mighty river. But You were with David when he slew the Philistines. You were with Samson when he brought the temple down on his enemies. You were with Joshua when he circled round the walls of Jericho and, with a blast on his trumpet, brought the walls down—with Your help, Heavenly Father! With Your Almighty help!

"I pray that You will be with us as we go out to do Your work. Come down this morning, Lawd, and kill these evil white people. We can't do it by ourselves. We are mere flesh. But You! You are all-powerful. Come down this morning and stand with us, Your people."

"Amen! Preach it, brother!"

"We ask these things in the name of Your son, Jesus. Amen."

"Amen!" all the men, except me, chorused.

"All right, my brothers. Let's move out. If we hurry we should be at our first stop just about the time the sun is waking up. We'll go by way of the road. Stay close to the side so that if patrollers come, we can move into the woods and hide until they've gone by. Now, my brothers! It is time to take our freedom!"

Gabriel motioned to me. "My son! Come! We will go together, you and I!"

I went and stood beside Gabriel, who hugged me tightly around the shoulders. "Today, my son, you become a man," he whispered. "I see you do not have a weapon. Do not worry. When the time comes, you can use my sword." Then, loudly: "Come, my brothers! God calls us to do His work!"

Gabriel moved quietly into the forest and along a path toward the road, me beside him, the others following. No one spoke.

Amma! Amma! I cried silently. *Where are you? Please show yourself! The mere sight of you would give me courage.*

But there was only the night and the whine of mosquitoes in the deep and dark silence.

Once we reached the road, we walked rapidly, one behind the other. The night was warm, but I don't think any of us noticed. I thought I detected fear among some of the men. It was one thing to dream about killing. It was entirely another to be setting out to do it. I could imagine some of the men wondering if things would be as Gabriel said. Would God take up a sword and help them slay their enemies? But what if God didn't? What if God was absent, as He seemed to be on every other occasion when one of them had called on His name? But no. We couldn't think like that. We wouldn't think at all. We would walk, one foot in front of the other. Walk, accompanied by the whine of mosquitoes. There was the occasional sound of someone slapping himself when bitten by one of the bloodsuckers, and the cries of tree frogs and crickets.

Suddenly, we heard another sound. Each of us heard it at practically the same instant, and without being told, we stood still as if we were one man.

There it was, slow, steady, the sound of hoofbeats. Far down the road we saw a faint yellow light bobbing in the darkness—a lantern carried by someone riding on horseback. Frantically, Gabriel motioned us to get into the woods. We did so, crouching behind the broad trunks of tall pine trees.

Closer and closer came the sound of the horse's hooves. We did not move. The horse's gait slowed, almost as if its rider were looking for someone. The mosquitoes swarmed around our ears, faces, and arms, whining and biting, but no one moved, cried out, or slapped at the bloodsucking insects.

The horseman was close enough now for us to make out the form of him and his horse. He slowed the horse even more as he came abreast of the spot where we had left the road. He raised the lantern high and peered into the woods. We lowered our heads as if that would somehow make us less visible. We held our breath and waited.

Then we heard the horse moving closer to the woods where we were. Suddenly, the rider slapped at his face and shouted, "Goddamn mosquitoes!" The horse neighed and reared as something bit it. The rider steadied the horse and pulled it back onto the road. "Goddamn it! Go suck somebody else's blood!" And kicking the horse in the flanks, he galloped away.

We did not move until we could no longer hear the horse's hooves on the road. Then Gabriel chuckled.

"My brothers! You see. The Lawd moves in mysterious and wondrous ways. It was God Almighty sent the mosquitoes to attack that white man and his horse. That was God's sign telling us that victory is assured."

Gabriel's words seemed to reassure the men, but I wondered: how can you tell when God is a mosquito and when He is Himself?

Night was beginning its retreat from day when we reached a large, two-story white house with a porch on three sides. In the rear, attached to the house by a passageway, was a smaller building, a wisp of smoke coming from its chimney. I recognized that as the kitchen.

Gabriel led us quietly onto the broad lawn facing the house to stand beneath the long limbs of an oak tree almost as old as all our ages combined. Ezekiel was by his side now.

"Wait here," Gabriel whispered to the men. Then he said to Ezekiel and me, "Let's go."

I followed them as they moved quickly to the rear of the house and into the kitchen.

A slave woman, who looked a lot like Harriet, was putting wood on a fire she had just started in the cookstove. She turned at the sound of the door opening, a smile on her face as if she knew who had just come in, but the smile vanished as the three of us stepped inside. Her eyes grew large when she saw the sword in Gabriel's hand.

"Good morning, auntie," he said.

"Who are you? What are you doing here? What do you want?" I heard the fear and panic in her voice.

"We've come to set you free!" Gabriel answered, and, smiling, he thrust the sword into her abdomen, pulled it out quickly, and thrust it in again. The woman moaned once and slowly slid to the floor, dead.

I gasped. "Why did you do that?"

"Because I had to, boy," Gabriel answered. "If I'd let her live, she would've gone and told the white folks."

"How do you know what she would have done?" I protested.

"Because she had that 'I love my white folks' look on her face like the one Sister Harriet has all the time."

All I had seen on her face was that she did not want to die. At that moment, I knew: no nyama would come that day. They would be too busy consoling the nyama Gabriel was unknowingly going to separate from the people they would no longer animate.

Gabriel drew the sword across his shirt, wiping it clean of blood as he looked contemptuously at me. "You want me to send you where I sent that white folks' nigger woman?"

I swallowed hard. "No," I managed to say.

"Then you best stop acting like a white folks' nigger." Gabriel turned and looked at Ezekiel, who was holding two long, thin pieces of burning logs he had taken from the stove.

"You ready?" Gabriel asked the blacksmith.

Ezekiel nodded.

"You want some help?" Gabriel asked.

"I got this. You keep an eye on him," he said, motioning with his head to me.

Gabriel smiled. "My boy is going to be all right."

Ezekiel pushed hard against the stove with his foot, knocking it over and spilling burning wood onto the floor. "You go on out front. The quarry won't be long in coming." And he hurried along the passageway into the main part of the house as the kitchen floor started to smolder.

I followed Gabriel to the lawn at the front of the house where the ten slaves waited under the oak tree. We watched silently as smoke began seeping from the house. Through the windows we could see Ezekiel working his way quickly from room to room, setting fire to drapes and anything else that would catch quickly. As Ezekiel came running out the front door, flames began leaping from the downstairs windows, and from upstairs came frightened voices yelling, "Fire! Fire!"

"All right!" Gabriel said. "Spread out as close to the house as you can get. Won't be long now."

Smoke billowed from the house as the flames inside got higher. Then we heard excited voices coming not from the house but from our left. We turned to see slaves running toward the back of the house, which was completely engulfed by fire.

"Mama! Mama!" came a man's voice. He was a big man, and several slaves had difficulty holding him back from running into what had been the kitchen.

I looked at Gabriel, hoping to see even the slightest

tinge of remorse or sorrow on his face, but his eyes were fixed on the front of the house as if nothing else existed. Just then, a white man and woman who looked vaguely familiar to me stumbled onto the porch, coughing from the smoke, running as fast as they could into the yard and away from the flames. As they staggered out of the smoke, Cato and two others grabbed them by the arms. The couple tried to pull away, but were flung to the ground.

"You know what to do!" Gabriel shouted.

The three hesitated. It seemed that thinking about killing white people was a lot easier than looking into their fearful eyes, hearing their rapid, shallow breathing, and smelling their fear.

"Kill them!" Gabriel shouted.

Cato, knife in hand, still did not move. Then he closed his eyes and plunged the knife into the bodies lying on the ground, first one and then the other, again and again. When he finished, his hands and arms were slick with blood, but he did not open his eyes until he got up and walked away. He never looked back at what he had done.

The kitchen at the back of the house collapsed into the flames. The slaves who had been standing nearby came to the edge of the front lawn. They stared, unbelieving, at us. I wondered what we looked like to them holding shovels, pitchforks, crude swords, and knives.

"Brothers! Sisters!" Gabriel called to them. "My name is Gabriel and I have come to bring you freedom." He moved toward them. "Come! Join me! We will go through the countryside and free the rest of our enslaved brothers and sisters! Join me! Join me!"

No one moved. Gabriel stopped as the slaves stared at him with a cold indifference, some with hostility even. The large, dark-skinned man, the son of the murdered cook, turned around and pointed at two boys. "Run to town and get the white folks! The rest of you men come with me!" They turned and walked away.

This was not the response Gabriel had expected. The slaves were supposed to come flocking to him because God was on his side. I watched him as he looked into the sky for the ram-headed God to be standing there, sword in His hand. But I could tell by the look of surprise and shock on Gabriel's face that there was nothing in the sky except what I saw, too—the pale oranges and reds of dawn.

"Here come the others!" Ezekiel exclaimed.

Gabriel turned to see a couple stagger onto the lawn.

"Yes!" he exclaimed.

"Kill the man and bring the woman to me!" he shouted. Immediately three men were on the man and killed him before he realized what was happening.

Gabriel then turned to me. "The time to prove yourself has come."

As two slaves brought the woman across the lawn, I recognized who it was. And everything became clear.

"Nathaniel?" Ellen asked, bewildered at seeing me. "Nathaniel," she said again, this time there was no question in her voice but only the love with which she had always infused my name since we were children.

"Ellen," I said, knowing that if I did anything to betray that love, I would be handing myself over to the chaos. But what else could I do? I began to call on Amma to save me, to save her, to take and deposit us somewhere far, far away as he had taken Josiah, Amina, and the seed that had been me from the docks of Charleston to that tiny island in less time than breath entered and flowed from the lungs. Just as Gabriel had searched the sky looking for the God who had promised to be with him, so I looked into the sky now. I saw only a dawn more beautiful than any I had ever seen.

"Nathaniel," she said again, not as a plea but as a statement of definition.

"Nathaniel," Gabriel repeated, his voice sharp with scorn. He held out his sword to me. "Kill her!" he commanded, and then added sarcastically, "Nathaniel."

I looked into Gabriel's eyes and saw a madness born from the inability to withstand pain. I knew what had been done to his brother by the word of a lying white woman, but that woman and this one were not the same. An unmistakable and undeniable "No!" welled up inside me with all the power of love.

I took the sword from Gabriel's outstretched hands. He smiled, and as he started to chuckle triumphantly, I lunged, and with more strength than I knew I had, I thrust the sword hard into Gabriel's stomach. The sword went in all the way to the hilt and through his small body.

Gabriel stared at me, his eyes large. His mouth opened to say something, but blood poured out instead of words. His hands clutched at the sword's handle, but there was no strength in his arms to pull it out. There was no longer strength in any part of his body, and slowly he sank to the ground, dead.

"I told him not to trust you, nigger!" Ezekiel shouted. "I

told him you was a white man's nigger! I told him. God damn it! You are not going to cheat me out of my revenge!"

I turned toward the sound of the voice coming from behind me, but Ezekiel was already rushing toward Ellen. Before I realized what was happening, the blacksmith had already plunged his sword into Ellen. She slumped to the ground, her eyes fixed on me, her mouth open. I knew she had been about to say that name one more time, but she was dead.

"We even now, Master Chelsea!" Ezekiel said, looking down at Ellen's body. "You took my daughter from me. I just took your daughter from you. We equal now. You and me. For the rest of your life, you gon' feel what I been feeling every day since you sent her and my grandbaby and your daughter away."

There came a great sound as the roof fell into the flaming remains of the house.

"Let's go!" I heard a voice shout.

I turned to see what must have been thirty to forty Foster plantation slaves coming toward us, armed with whatever they felt they could use as weapons—rakes, shovels, whips, and sticks.

"This is what I was trying to tell Gabriel," George said to no one in particular. "The niggers on this plantation weren't ready for freedom. I told Gabriel this morning, told him this was the wrong place to start. Not only were these niggers not ready to be free, this plantation is too close to town." Then he looked at me. "It's your fault. We were supposed to kill Master Chelsea first, then go to the Wilson plantation. But for some reason I don't understand, Gabriel got the idea in his head to come here so that you could kill

Miss Ellen. But you went and killed him rather than kill a white woman! My sister's a fool to love you!"

Ezekiel, George, Cato, and the others were surrounded quickly by the Foster plantation slaves and relieved of their weapons. No one resisted. They let themselves be taken as if they had just awoken from a long and heavy sleep and were still too groggy to know clearly where they were and what they had done.

I was not bothered. The large, dark-skinned man came over to me and said, "Go. My sister and some of the others seen what you did. You was the only one what killed some-body that needed killing. I sent a couple of the older boys to town to fetch the white folks. I expect they be here pretty soon. You get on away from here. You don't belong with the rest of these niggers. You go on now."

I looked to where Ellen lay on the ground, her ab-domen soaked with blood. With tears in my eyes, I left. When I reached the road I started running as fast as I could, wishing I could run away from what I had seen and what I had done—and not done. My chest was burning as if it had been set afire, but I did not stop. I ran, my face drenched with tears like blood. I ran, sobbing, stumbling as my legs refused to carry me as fast as I wanted them to.

When I reached the woods of the Chelsea plantation, I started to scream. In and out, in and out, the screams came with each breath. Later, Sylvie told me that my screams were so loud that people were afraid their eardrums were going to shatter and they put their hands over their ears. All I remember is stumbling onto the lane of the slave quarters and seeing Sylvie running toward me as fast as she could.

PART THREE

1

The slaves on the Chelsea plantation had known something was supposed to happen that morning, but not what. Every day for months, Gabriel had been talking about God ordering him to kill white people, his arms moving around like a man who couldn't swim trying to keep himself from drowning. They had noticed small groups of men talking quietly with one another, as if they had a secret they couldn't share. Some of the slaves swore that any time they heard the "owl" give its three calls, they could feel evil swirling around their cabins like a lonely wind looking for something to destroy.

Sylvie had known exactly what was going to happen that morning. George had told her how Gabriel had changed the plan and, instead of killing Master Chelsea first and then going to the plantations farthest from town, Gabriel was going to the Foster place first.

"That don't make sense," George told her. "What he want to attack the plantation closest to town for?"

Sylvie knew why Gabriel had changed his mind, but she said nothing to her brother. Then, last night, when she heard the "owl," she wanted to go with George and tell Gabriel she was sorry, that she had not meant what she said, that she had not heard Nat and Ellen say they loved each other, that she had been hurting then but now she wasn't hurting so bad. However, when she heard George get up and leave, she did not stir. She did not fall back asleep either.

Instead, she went outside, sat on the ground in front of the cabin, and waited. She didn't know what she was waiting for, but she knew she was waiting for something and it wouldn't be good.

False dawn came. Then first light. She heard stirring from the other cabins as slaves awoke to begin another day no different from all the ones before. Or so they thought. The sun had just cleared the horizon, and slaves were trudging slowly from their cabins toward the field when they heard screaming from deep in the woods. Although Sylvie had never heard a sound like that, she knew who it came from. And because the pain in that scream almost shattered her heart, she knew what had happened.

Now that Miss Ellen was dead, Sylvie did not know how she could live with herself. When she lied to Gabriel, she had not thought about how much Nat would be hurt by Miss Ellen's death. Only now did Sylvie understand: the pain you felt when somebody died was just another way of feeling how much you loved them. Nat's screams said that it did not matter that Miss Ellen was dead; his love for her was more alive than ever.

But Sylvie ran to him anyway, reaching him just as he came out of the woods. He continued his stumbling, staggering run through the slave quarters, Sylvie by his side. Suddenly, he stopped and let out a scream so loud that someone later said it caused a crack in the sky. Then he slumped to the ground. Sylvie motioned for someone to help her carry him into Sister Harriet's cabin, and there they laid him on his bed.

All through the morning Sylvie sat beside the bed and wiped his face with cool compresses. But as quickly as she wiped away the perspiration, more appeared. His skin was so hot that it almost burned her fingers to touch him. Occasionally he mumbled something, but Sylvie couldn't understand the words. Not that she tried too hard. She was afraid to hear what he might say, afraid to learn what had happened to him and the others.

That afternoon, they learned what happened. White men came riding into the slave quarters, twelve of them. Tied to the horses and being dragged behind were the bodies of Gabriel and the men who had been with him.

Sylvie saw George, and bit her lip to keep from crying aloud.

"Oh, Lawd, Lawd, Lawd!" Sister Harriet muttered, turning her head away.

"That's Ezekiel," someone whispered, pointing to a stocky, bloody figure being dragged behind a white horse ridden by a tall white man with a drooping mustache framing his thin lips.

"That look like Cato."

"Ain't that Darius?"

"There's Gabriel!"

"Oh, Lawd Jesus! That's Little Sam!"

Heads turned to look at Big Sam and Cleora, and they

were surprised to see a look of almost pride on their faces, even though they were crying.

Back and forth, back and forth the bodies were dragged between the facing rows of cabins that made up the slave quarters. The slaves understood: this is what will happen to you if you dare to raise your hand against a white man or woman.

Finally, the men on their horses began leaving. The man on the last horse turned around and yelled, "If you want the bodies to bury, you can fish them out of the river."

A great wailing noise went up from the slaves as they thought about their husbands, sons, and brothers lying in the dark and muddy depths of the river being eaten by fish. For many years afterward, none of the blacks in that area fished or ate fish.

———

Though it may have looked like I was unconscious, I was aware of Sylvie and Harriet's presence, of them taking turns wiping the sweat from my face. I heard the sounds of the horses as they went back and forth through the slave quarters. Though my eyes were closed, I could see the bodies being dragged along the ground. Even though the men were dead, I felt pain as stones stabbed and earth tore bloodied skin. Though my eyes were closed, I wept, but I didn't know for whom I wept more—Ellen, who had been killed, Gabriel, whom I had killed, or all the others who had died that morning. Over and over in my mind I saw myself taking the proffered sword from Gabriel, feeling its heft as my fingers curved around the handle, and then lunging and driving the blade into and through Gabriel's body. I could still see the look of a father's perverse pride on Gabriel's face turn quickly to one of surprise and then hopelessness as he realized that his death was from the hand of his son.

I had not thought beforehand about what to do. I had done the only thing I could have. I killed Gabriel to save Ellen. Except I hadn't. I had only saved myself.

As I lay there, I wondered if I should have told Master Chelsea that Gabriel was planning an uprising. I had known that Gabriel's words meant death, not freedom. If I had done something, Ellen would still be alive. And maybe all the others as well. Master Chelsea would have sold them, of course, but they would still be alive. But was life as a slave better than death? I didn't have an answer.

It was toward evening when I heard Sylvie leave. I opened my eyes and found myself looking up into Harriet's anxious face.

"Didn't know if you was going to wake up or not," she said. "How you feel?"

"Tired," I said softly. "Very tired."

"Let me make you a cup of tea."

"It's not that kind of tired. I'm weary in my soul."

"You was there, weren't you?"

I nodded. "I killed Gabriel."

Harriet was silent for a moment. Then she asked, "When you say 'I killed Gabriel,' was it you who did it, or was it my Nat?"

"I did it." I paused. "Nat will not be coming back," I added softly.

Harriet nodded. "Ever since you told me about the . . . what do you call it?"

"Nyama."

"Ever since you told me about it, I had a feeling I wasn't going to be with him again."

"I'm sorry."

"That's all right. I always thought he had only one foot in this world. He was a sweet boy but not a strong one. He didn't have the spirit to withstand all a person has to go through in slavery. He was like his father in that way."

I sat up, startled by what she said. "What do you mean?"

"Gabriel used to tell me to my face that I wasn't nothing but a 'white folks' nigger.' I can understand why I looked that way to him. But looks ain't always truth. What Gabriel couldn't understand was how much strength it takes to be a slave and to care about the one who's keeping you a slave. Gabriel didn't have the spirit for that. He didn't have the spirit to withstand the temptation to hate. And Nat? He wasn't brave enough to love. If you're not careful, slavery will reduce you to being what they want you to be, and all they want is for you to make them the most important thing in your life. But if you goin' to survive in slavery, you got to find the way to do what's most important for your own self, for your nyama, I guess you would say. Gabriel got caught up in hating white people, and that didn't do his nyama a bit of good. Nat got caught up in the fear to love. He didn't know, and I couldn't tell him, that he should have let himself love Ellen, even if it meant the white folks would hang him from a tree."

"But that day in the kitchen, the day Ellen came to see Nat, you told him to be careful. You said he had to have enough sense for him and Ellen."

"I know and I'm sorry. My mouth said what my head was thinking, not what my heart was feeling. I haven't always had as much courage as I would have liked, but at least I always knew when I had failed. Neither Gabriel or Nat ever knew when they had failed themselves.

"Like Master Chelsea. He sitting in that big ol' house by himself this morning and he's finding out how much he's failed himself."

"What do you mean?"

Harriet shook her head. "Ain't for me to say. But I know the lie he been living." She sighed. "What you gon' do now? You goin' back to Africa?"

"No. I haven't done what I was brought here to do. But I still don't know how to do it. I don't know why I thought Gabriel's way was the path."

"Don't feel bad. Gabriel believed evil was good. That made him no different than all these white folks who believe keeping us as slaves is good." She got up. "You sure you don't want nothin'?"

"Thank you, but I'm sure."

"Well, I best be getting on over to the big house. Master Chelsea don't need to be sitting there by himself. If you feel up to it, you can come on to the house 'round the usual time. I'll have supper ready. If not, I'll bring you something tonight."

"I think I'll stay here."

"That's all right, son. I'll bring you something later."

"Thank you, Harriet."

———

She had not been gone long before the door opened slowly. It was Sylvie.

"You awake?" she asked shyly. "I was worried about you," she said, sitting on the bed next to me.

"I think I'm all right," I responded.

Sylvie took my hand and put her fingers through it. I turned to look at her. She was staring down at our interlaced hands and I couldn't help remembering the last time someone had taken my hand and held it in hers and stared at them. It seemed as if there was something Sylvie wanted to say but didn't know how.

I waited. Finally, she looked at me. "There's something I have to tell you, and I'll understand if you don't want to have anything to do with me after you hear what it is."

There was another long silence as tears came into her eyes. "It was all my fault," she said in a small voice.

"What was your fault?"

"What happened. George told me that Gabriel's plan was to go against Master Chelsea first. But after I told him about you and Master Chelsea's daughter, he changed his plans."

"What did you tell him?" I asked.

Sylvie squeezed my hand tightly. "Late one afternoon when I was leaving the field, I decided to go down to the carpentry shed to see you. You'd been acting a little strange, like you didn't care about Sylvie anymore. When I got there, I heard a woman's voice and I knew who it was. I couldn't hear anything either one of you said, but I was so mad that I went and told Gabriel that I heard you and her saying how much you loved each other."

"That was a lie!" I exclaimed. Not really, I added silently. Although Sylvie had not heard us say the words, she had perceived the truth.

Sylvie started to cry. "I know it was. I know it was. But I was just so mad. Ever since I can remember, it seemed like she was always with you. I wanted to be the one playing with you, the one sitting back of the barn. But I was out there in the field working in the hot sun. When she went away, I thought I would finally have you to myself. But I didn't. She wasn't here, but that didn't keep you from thinking about her. She was supposed to be getting married, but there she was in the shed with you. What was black Sylvie supposed to think? When I told Gabriel that Master Chelsea's daughter was with you, he said that the white woman is the worst thing on the face of the earth. He said he didn't understand how a son of his could prefer a white girl to a beautiful black girl like me. He said killing a white woman would do more to bring down slavery than anything else.

"George told me that him and Ezekiel tried their best to get Gabriel to go back to the original plan. They said it was too dangerous to attack the Foster plantation because it was too close to town, that they would be caught before they got started good. George told him that the Foster plantation niggers were too scared to rise up, but the ones on the Wilson plantation, five miles on the other side of this plantation, they were ready. Master Wilson treated his mules better than he did his niggers. But nothing they said could get Gabriel to change his mind."

"Killing Ellen was more important to him than freedom."

"I'm sorry, Nat. I'm so sorry. It was all my fault. Please forgive me. I'll do anything if you will forgive me."

I took my hand away and stared at her. "I'm sorry," I said. "I'm not the one who can forgive you. Only Ellen and the twelve who died can do that."

"But they're dead," Sylvie said, bursting into tears again. "How can they forgive me?"

"I don't know."

"Are you angry with me?"

I did not want to hurt her any more than she was already hurting. But neither would I lie to her. "Am I angry with you?" I repeated her question. "When you told Gabriel that you heard me and Ellen talking about how much we loved each other, that was like taking a man who had a loaded pistol in his hand and pointing his arm in the direction you wanted him to shoot. You knew what you were doing when you told Gabriel about me and Ellen." I stopped to let my growing anger subside. "You should go. Maybe we can talk more at another time, but for right now, I think you should go."

Sylvie hesitated, then got up and went out the door, crying softly.

2

That night, as I lay in bed, eyes open, the giant bird of night-black feathers came through the ceiling for the first time since it had brought my nyama and placed it in Nat's body.

"Amma!" I exclaimed, tears coming to my eyes.

The bird rested on my chest and stared at me with tiny round yellow eyes.

I was wrong to have brought you here. There is no hope for this land. It is best to leave and let the nyama of all the dead here do with this land as they wish. I have come to take your nyama home to Africa.

The bird's talons tightened as they prepared to reach inside and take out my nyama. I put my hand atop the talons to relax them.

My nyama is not the same. It has absorbed the nyama that resided in this body, the nyama of the one called Nat.

The bird turned its head to the left and then to the right, as if trying to understand what I had just said.

So? Your nyama is powerful. His was weak.

Yes, but there is a part of the nyama which I absorbed which I am not wholly in control of.

How could that be?

I am not sure. Nat kept a part of his nyama hidden from himself. These were feelings so powerful he was afraid of them. These feelings had an entirely different name, and when someone spoke that name, the emotions came to life because my nyama was strong enough to withstand them.

What is this emotion called?

It appears to be a combination of love and devotion.

The bird ruffled its black feathers as if needing to shed itself of insects only it knew burrowed within. *So. You will bring this love and devotion to Africa.*

What if I do not wish to return? What if I want to stay here and find the way to do what you brought me here to do?

You are choosing to stay here and be a slave?

I won't be a slave much longer. There is a war coming that will end slavery.

And then what? Do you think the evil white people of this land will see the beauty and dignity of black people?

Some will. Most won't. But it does not matter.

I will not come for you again. If you do not come with me now, you are doomed to live out your days here.

I know.

The bird stared at me. *You have chosen your fate. You are condemned to this land and its people, all of them.*

I am Nathaniel now. I cannot leave.

I weep for you. And the bird spread its wings and was gone.

3

The following morning the plantation was eerily quiet. There were no sounds of doors opening and closing, no sounds of talking as slaves got ready for the day. Occasionally there came the sound of crying or a muffled scream from one of the cabins. But that was all.

Death lay not only over the Chelsea plantation but over the entire land for miles around. White men and white women looked at their slaves with different eyes, wondering which ones were plotting to kill them. But they couldn't know just by looking, so they decided that all slaves might be thinking about killing them.

When people are afraid, they will strike what they fear before it can strike them. So it was that morning, and on many plantations, slaves were beaten and a few were killed, not because of anything they had done but because of what white people *thought* they might be thinking about doing.

Ekundayo and Harriet had not been out of bed long before the door of their cabin opened. They turned to see Master Chelsea walk in.

"Morning, Harriet. Morning, Nat," he greeted them quietly, his head down.

If Harriet and Ekundayo had not known better, they would have thought he was a beggar. His dark hair lay in a tangled mass atop his head. He was unshaven and a stubble of white beard covered his cheeks, chin, and upper lip in stark contrast to the dark hair of his head. The brown pants, white shirt, and brown coat he had on were dirty and wrinkled. He looked like a man whom life had broken into small pieces and showed no interest in putting back together again.

"Morning, Master Chelsea," Harriet said. "You come on in and sit here." She pointed to one of the chairs at the table.

Ekundayo motioned Harriet to sit in the other chair on the side of the table opposite Master Chelsea. He sat on the edge of his bed.

"I heard what you did," Master Chelsea said to Nat.

"Suh?"

"From the way some of the slaves at the Foster plantation described the man who killed Gabriel, I knew it was you. They said if it wasn't for you, no telling what would have happened. Your killing Gabriel seemed to have taken the starch out of the rest. It takes a brave man to kill his own father to keep his father from doing wrong. A brave man."

Ekundayo didn't know what to say, so he said nothing.

"I'm grateful to you, and everybody on the plantation should be grateful to you. The other slave owners in the area were ready to come over and kill every slave here since all of the twelve had come from this plantation. The only thing that stopped them was hearing what you had done, that you had come along with Gabriel and the others hoping to find a way to put a stop to all the killing they were planning to do."

That wasn't how it was. But sometimes truth was not what happened but what someone needed to believe happened.

"I'm a ruined man in the community. The other owners and all the upstanding white folks of the area have made it clear they want nothing to do with me. They've always thought I treated my slaves too well, treated them like they were human beings. And look what happened. I don't understand. I let Ezekiel hire out his time to whoever could pay the most for his services. He thanks me by killing my daughter?"

There was a long silence. Finally, Ekundayo said, "He said something about you selling away his daughter. He said he wanted you to feel what it was like to lose your only child."

Tears came into Samuel Chelsea's eyes. "Well, he succeeded."

"He also said something about you selling his grandbaby and your baby," Ekundayo continued softly.

Samuel flinched like he had just been slapped. "Well, I reckon I can understand Ezekiel. I can even understand Gabriel after what happened to his brother. But that don't explain the others. Big Sam runs this place. Why would his boy get mixed up in something like this? And Cato? Every day he had a joke to tell me, or a new tale he had made up. I treat you all better than any slave owner in the state of Virginia. You all was damn near free!"

"Damn near free is just another way of being a slave," Ekundayo responded quietly.

He and Samuel Chelsea stared at each other for a moment.

"That's what Ellen used to say to me," Samuel said, looking away from Ekundayo's piercing eyes. The white man started to cry but, embarrassed, caught himself. He sniffed loudly a couple of times, wiped his eyes, then stood up. "That's not why I come down here. I'm burying Ellen this afternoon. I come to ask if you wouldn't mind saying a few words over her, Nat. I know she would like that. Won't be nobody there 'cepting us three. None of my so-called friends want anything to do with me, and the slaves didn't know her. I'd be obliged if you and Harriet would come and if you would say something."

Ekundayo nodded. "I'd be pleased to."

"I appreciate it." He turned to Harriet. "You don't need to come to the house today. I won't be eating breakfast. I don't know if I'll ever eat again."

"Don't say that, Master Chelsea. I be to the house directly. I reckon I should start packing away the things Miss Ellen left here before she moved to the Foster place."

"I appreciate it, Harriet. I can't even go in her room."

"Don't you worry about it none. Harriet will take care of everything."

Ekundayo and Harriet were quiet for a moment after Master Chelsea left.

"I feel sorry for him," Harriet said eventually.

"How do you feel about Ezekiel and Gabriel and all the rest who were killed yesterday?"

"You don't think I feel sorry for them, too?" Harriet shot back.

"Just asking."

"I feel sorry for all them I be hearing crying way up in the night, all the mothers and wives and sisters. But as for Gabriel and the rest of 'em? They brought trouble on themselves."

"So they deserved what happened to 'em?"

"Don't nobody deserve to die, but if you pick up a rattlesnake, you shouldn't be surprised when he bites you and fills you full of poison. Why you asking me all these questions? I should be asking you. Do you feel sorry for them? Do you think they got what they deserved?"

Ekundayo sighed. "I don't know what I feel. I was asking you because maybe knowing what you felt would help me figure out what I feel."

"Us ain't supposed to have too many feelings, especially ones the white folks don't want us to have."

"Like anger and hatred and wanting to be free?"

—

I went to the burying ground early. It was behind a line of tall pine trees near the barn. At one end of the field were the graves of Charlotte Ramsey Chelsea and her parents, grandparents, and great-grandparents. At the head of each grave was a stone on which was carved the name and dates of birth and death of the one who lay beneath. Next to Charlotte's grave was a deep oblong hole, a mound of dirt beside it, and two long pieces of rope atop the hill of earth.

Slaves were buried at the other end of the field. No stones stood at the heads of these graves. I walked over the field, certain I was walking on many of the dead, because the only way to recognize a possible grave was if an oblong piece of earth was sunken in. I wondered who lay beneath this ground and what their lives had been like. Though they had lived and died as slaves, that was not the sum of their lives. Even within the confines of slavery, there were times of joy and peace and contentment, small moments in which one stood outside one's definition as a slave and became, simply, a man or a woman. Such moments gave shape and texture and color to one's nyama, as surely as how one faced the challenges diminished the quality of an nyama. I hoped that those who lay there had been able to squeeze enough moments of joy from the bitterness of slavery to know that they were not what white people said they were.

The sun was more than half the way of its journey to the western horizon when I saw four slaves walking toward the burying ground, a coffin on their shoulders, a coffin I had made, as Samuel Chelsea and Harriet walked slowly behind.

I took the two lengths of rope, straightened them, and laid them on the ground. The slaves put the pine box gently atop the ropes and then stepped to the side. For a long moment, Samuel Chelsea stared at the wooden box which held his daughter's body. Tears flowed freely down his face as he said, over and over, "I'm sorry. I am so sorry."

Harriet moved to his side and took his arm, saying, "Now. Now. She's in a better place, a better place."

He nodded but without conviction.

I looked down at the unadorned pine box, its cover

nailed tightly. For a moment I was afraid I was going to give way to grief, but then I thought about the woman lying in the darkness of the coffin, and I smiled.

"I'm glad I had the chance to know you," I began. "You didn't let yourself be fooled into believing that a person's skin color told you anything about him. That was true when you looked at me. It was true when you looked in the mirror. You didn't let yourself be fooled into believing that your white skin told you anything about who you were. There wasn't much of a place in the world for a person like you. You were living in a world we haven't made yet. You were living in a world nobody even knows how to make. But perhaps that's what you came to show us. If you want the world to be a certain way, you have to live that way.

"We are going to put your body in this hole in the ground, but your spirit—and that's who you really were— your spirit is right here next to my heartbeat. Thank you for being among us. Thank you for showing us that we can be more than we think we can."

I looked at the four slaves standing a little distance away. They came forward and, taking the ropes, lifted the coffin, then slowly lowered it into the grave. Samuel Chelsea was sobbing uncontrollably now as Harriet started singing:

Soon one morning,
Death come creeping in my room.
Soon one morning,
Death come creeping in my room.

Soon one morning,
Death come creeping in my room.
Oh my Lord! Oh my Lord!
What will I do?

I took a shovel from the mound of dirt and turned a handful into the grave. The dirt made a hollow sound as it fell onto the pine box, a sound that caused Master Chelsea to let out a scream and run toward the grave as if he were going to jump in. But two of the slaves caught him and held him back. Harriet took him by the arm and slowly led him away from the grave and back toward the big house.

I thanked the slaves for digging the grave and carrying the coffin. "You can go on. I'll fill it in."

"We don't mind helping," one of them offered.

"I know you don't, brother, and I appreciate it. But I'd like to do it myself."

They nodded as if they understood and left.

Alone now, I cried as I put each shovelful of earth onto the coffin. I worked slowly, my tears dropping onto the dirt as it went into the hole.

Eventually the grave was filled. With the back of the shovel I smoothed the mound of earth until it was neat and symmetrical. I could feel Nat's sorrow at never telling her that he loved her, his sorrow that he had been afraid to kiss her, his sorrow that he had lacked the courage to join his spirit with hers, even if it had meant his death. How beautiful his nyama would have been if he had allowed himself his audacious love. But now I would have to live with his pain for the rest of my life.

As I turned to leave, I thought I saw someone in the late afternoon shadows near the barn. It was Sylvie. As I came closer, she started toward me but walked past and went and knelt at Ellen's grave, her lips moving as if she were praying.

I waited for her, and when she finished, she came to where I was standing. We walked in silence past the barn and toward the slave quarters.

Finally, she said, "I told her how sorry I was for what I did. I asked her to forgive me. Do you think she did?"

I did not answer. Instead, I took Sylvie's hand, and we walked on—together.

4

Mornings began in silence now. It was as if a shroud had been placed over the plantation. People stared blankly, their minds still seeing the bodies of the twelve being dragged back and forth, back and forth. Some said that at night they heard moans coming from the woods toward the river where the bodies were thrown.

I had not heard anything, but I did not doubt those who said they had. The nyama belonging to the twelve must be in great pain. That was how it was with those who died violently. I wished I knew what to do for them.

I got out of bed, took the bucket, and went to the well to fill it. When I came back, Harriet was up.

"Did you sleep?" she asked.

"Not much."

"Me neither. I don't think anybody on the plantation has been sleeping much. What's gon' become of us?"

"What do you mean?" I asked.

"The sorrow is so thick around here, I'm afraid it's going to settle into my bones. Nobody's got enough tears for all the sorrow they feeling. I know I don't. And Master Chelsea. Lawd, have mercy! The grief is about to make him crazy!"

As if he had been summoned, the door opened and Samuel Chelsea walked in. He was wearing the same clothes he'd had on the day before and the day before that. The white stubble on his face was thicker. With eyes cast down, he sat in the chair at the table where he'd sat before. Harriet beckoned for me to sit in the chair on the other side, but I shook my head and gestured for her to sit there. She refused and, reluctantly, I took the place opposite Samuel Chelsea while Harriet made herself comfortable on the edge of her bed.

None of us said anything for a long while. Finally, Samuel raised his head and stared into the cold fireplace. "I think children sometimes live out things the parents didn't live out for themselves." He turned and looked at me. Then he looked at Harriet and smiled sadly. "How did you know I was coming to talk to him?" he asked her.

"I didn't. I was just hoping."

Samuel nodded slowly, then turned back to me. "About a week before her wedding, Ellen came to me and asked me to free you and give her enough money so you and she could get to Canada. If I had said yes, she'd be alive today, alive for many years to come. But I didn't. I couldn't. I know she thought my refusal had something to do with that I couldn't see my daughter being with a black man. That was part of it, but not all." He stopped and turned his head to gaze once again into the cold fireplace.

"I have never told anybody what I'm about to tell you. Maybe saying it aloud will bring some peace to my soul. But I doubt it. I don't think I'll have a moment of peace ever again, but maybe telling you my story will make me a little less alone." He cleared his throat, wiped at his eyes, and began.

"As Harriet knows, this plantation belonged to Charlotte's father, Octavius Ramsey, and to his father before. Octavius was a lawyer, and I was a clerk in his office. For whatever reasons, he took a liking to me. My father was a doctor who died when I was seventeen. My mother died about six months later. Octavius started inviting me out to the plantation for dinner on Sundays. That's when I got to know Charlotte. She was Octavius's only child, and he didn't want to entrust her with the great plantation he and his father had built. One day he asked me what I thought of Charlotte. I thought she was attractive but a little on the homely side. There wasn't much fire in her personality and I told him. He said he was aware of that, and he was afraid he wouldn't be able to marry her off to someone who wouldn't take advantage of her. Then he told me that if I married her, the plantation would be mine when he died."

Samuel stopped and sighed deeply. "My parents hadn't left me anything when they died. Even the house I'd grown up in belonged to the bank, and they took it over when I couldn't make the payments. I had nothing, and here was this man I respected and looked up to telling me that the Ramsey plantation could be mine if I married his daughter. A chance like that might come along once in a lifetime, if you were lucky. So I told him yes.

"We agreed that Charlotte must never know, that I would have to woo her and win her hand. That wasn't hard to do. Suitors were not lined up to see her. So I courted her, knowing that Charlotte would have married the first man who paid attention to her.

"I liked her well enough, but I didn't love her. I acted as if I did, however, said all the things women like to hear, gave her nice things, married her, and hoped she would never know the truth.

"One day, I rode out to the field to discuss something with the overseer. Don't remember what it was and it's not important now. What's important is that my eyes happened to light on a slave girl. It was Ezekiel's daughter, though I didn't know that at the time, and it wouldn't have made any difference if I had. I looked at her and it felt like my heart left my body and went to her so it could beat alongside hers. She was beautiful, with large, dark eyes and full lips. There was a soft sweetness about her that touched my soul.

"I suppose if I had been content to abide by the mores of the South, everything would have been fine. Practically every white man of standing in the county availed himself of pretty black girls whenever he wanted. But I was in love with Susannah. It was not only the sexual part. Whenever I was with her, I felt like I was myself. We laughed together. Even though she couldn't read or write, she had no trouble understanding whatever I talked about, whether it was some problem on the plantation or some business matter. I hated that she was a slave. I hated slavery and everything that went along with it. This illiterate black slave was more of a woman than white and educated Charlotte would ever be. If I had had the money, I would have bought Susannah's freedom and gone off to Canada with her. But I had nothing of my own.

"Then the oddest thing happened. Charlotte and I had been trying to have a baby for the almost two years we'd been married. After my passion was awakened by Susannah, Charlotte became pregnant. Octavius was thrilled that he was going to have a grandchild. I should have been happy, too, but I wasn't. I wanted Susannah to have my baby. I became more distant from Charlotte than ever. She may have been homely but she wasn't dumb. She knew something had changed in me, because I stopped even pretending that there was any kind of emotional bond between us. My passion belonged to Susannah, and that was not only my sexual passion but my heart's passion.

"One night, Charlotte asked me why I had married her. I knew I was supposed to say it was because I loved her and wanted to make a life with her. But I couldn't. The silence got deeper and deeper. Charlotte broke it and wanted to know if her father had promised me the plantation if I married her. My silence was enough of an answer. She cried for a little while, and when she dried her eyes, the tears were replaced by a look of hatred I undoubtedly deserved.

"But I didn't care, because it was around this time that Susannah became pregnant. I was ecstatic! She and Charlotte gave birth within weeks of each other, and both gave birth to daughters. I was not unhappy when Ellen was born, but I was delirious with joy when Susannah gave birth. I named the child Miranda, and I didn't hide from anyone that I was the proud father. That was another breach of Southern mores. It was all right for a white man to have as many children by slave girls as he wanted, as long as he didn't claim them as his own. But I did not hide my visits to the slave quarters to see Susannah and Miranda.

"One day, Octavius called me into the study. He told me that Southern white women expected their husbands to consort with slave women and even give them babies. According to him, this kind of behavior had the approval of white women because they were spared having a man's sexual needs imposed on them. He said a white woman was content to look the other way as long as her husband was discreet. Unfortunately, I was not being discreet.

"He asked me how I felt about Susannah. I told him the truth: I loved her. He told me that if he'd known I was such a fool, he would never have suggested that I court Charlotte, and he certainly would not have agreed to my inheriting the plantation. He gave me an ultimatum: sell Susannah and the baby, or give up Charlotte and my claim to the plantation."

Samuel shook his head slowly. "My God!" he exclaimed, his voice breaking. "I still don't believe the choice I made. I still don't believe that the very next day I told Susannah that I was going to have to sell her and Miranda. She spit in my face. I tried to explain; I wanted her to understand. How foolish that was. How was she supposed to understand that the man who had told her countless times how much he loved her was going to sell her to the highest bidder?

"I took her into Richmond to the slave market and

handed her over to the auctioneer. There was more bidding for her than any other slave put on the block that day. As I said, Susannah was very beautiful, and my heart sank when a man bought her who had nothing but lust in his eyes. I knew what lay ahead for her.

"A few months went by and I got a letter from the man who had bought her. He was demanding his money back. Susannah had drowned herself and Miranda in a river. But I knew: I had killed her soul. I suppose I should have told Ezekiel what happened to his daughter and granddaughter, but what difference would it have made? Selling his daughter and"—he stopped and then continued—"and grandbaby had already been like death for him."

He stopped again and sighed deeply. "Well, I suppose my father-in-law and my wife thought that with Susannah gone, I would come to my senses. Just the reverse happened. With Susannah gone, I went into a deep depression. I couldn't eat. I couldn't sleep. I was quite pathetic, so pathetic that Octavius had nothing but contempt for me.

"One day, he asked me if I was still pining over that 'nigger gal.' I told him her name was Susannah and that I would love her until my dying day. He got furious. I could see the veins popping out on his head. I left the study and went out to the porch to give him a chance to cool down. Instead, he came tearing after me and started calling me all kinds of fools. He was yelling and screaming and told me to get the hell out of his house, that I would never inherit his plantation. His face got real red, and then he started pulling at the collar of his shirt and gasping for breath. The next thing I knew, he fell to the porch."

Samuel paused. "This is the part I've never told anyone. Harriet, I know you knew about me and Susannah, but what you didn't know was that Octavius didn't die at once. He lay there on the porch looking at me, pulling at that collar on his shirt. He seemed surprised that I wasn't moving to help him. What did he think? If he lived, I would be out on the road without a penny to my name. I couldn't let that happen. It seemed to take forever before Octavius stopped making those gurgling sounds and his body relaxed. But eventually it did. I checked his pulse. He was dead.

"Then I went upstairs and told Charlotte. She looked at me like I had killed him myself, and I had. But being civilized people, Charlotte and I settled into living together after the mourning period ended. I thought everything was all right, as all right as things could be when two people lived together without love between them.

"One day, Charlotte told me she was going into Richmond to visit with some of her lady friends. The next day, a lawyer I knew in Richmond came out and told me that Charlotte's body had just been fished out of the James River. She had killed herself rather than continue living with me."

He looked at me. "Do you understand now why I tried to keep you and Ellen apart? I didn't want her to succeed where I had failed. I didn't want her to have the love in her life that I had thrust away from my own. How selfish can a man be?" He shook his head. "You may think there is nothing worse than physical slavery, and maybe there isn't. But at this minute, I would swap places with either one of you. The question is: would you swap places with me?"

Neither Harriet nor I spoke, but we didn't have to. Samuel Chelsea saw the pity for him on Harriet's face and the contempt on mine.

"I don't blame you," Samuel said finally. "I don't want to be me either."

The three of us sat in silence for a long while. What could we say in response to a life that had been lived poorly and without honesty? Samuel Chelsea had failed to be a decent human being, which was a failure of the most elemental kind.

"I've heard that it's never too late to change," Samuel said, breaking the silence. "I don't know if that's true. But I'm going to give it a try. I'm going to do what my daughter always wanted me to do. I've decided to free the slaves. I'm sorry it took Ellen's death to make me do something that would have made her happy. Nat, I'd appreciate it if you'd go to all the cabins in the quarters and tell the slaves to come to the big house. But before you go, I just want you to know that I hope you stay. You're my only link to my daughter. And, Harriet, I can't imagine this place without you."

It didn't take long for the slaves to assemble on the grass before the front porch. Samuel Chelsea ran a hand nervously through his hair several times and then began speaking.

"I don't quite know what to say. I've always tried to be

a good master to you. But I guess there can't be no such thing as a good master. A slave master is a slave master, and there ain't no good to be found in that. So I've decided to stop owning slaves. I'm setting you free. As of this minute, you're as free as any white man. You can stay here, and I'll pay you as good a wage as I can. And to tell the truth, I need you to stay. I can't work this place by myself. If you stay, I'll pay you just as I would pay a white man. But if you want to go, I understand. However, if you go, you're on your own.

"There's one other thing you should know. There's a war coming between them who've got slaves and them who don't, that being the South and the North. If the North wins, slavery is finished. If the South wins, slavery will be with us for a long time to come. If I was a slave, I reckon I'd strike out right now and head west where there ain't never been slavery, someplace like Nebraska or Kansas, or the Indian territories."

"How we gon' go somewhere if we ain't got cash money?" Big Sam asked, angry.

"If I had some money to give you, Sam, I would do it. I'm rich in land and rich in slaves, but I don't have much in the way of cash. I wish I did. Maybe you should stay a while, save whatever money you can, and then take your freedom. Of course, anybody who stays will have to pay rent on their cabin and the little garden patches you have around your houses, and you'll have to pay me for whatever food I give you."

"We can't do that if we ain't got money," someone else pointed out.

"I understand that. Them that wants to stay, can, and I'll deduct money for rent and food from what I'll pay you. Won't be much, 'cause I ain't got a lot. And one other thing. Them that decides to take their freedom will need a piece of paper from me saying they are free. That won't guarantee that folks will believe it, or respect it. Some white man might tear up your freedom papers and say you were his runaway, and there wouldn't be a judge that would dispute it. But once you get out of Virginia, you'll be in free territory. Them that wants to be free can come around the back of the house and I'll make out your free papers."

No one moved. I knew they were wondering the same thing I was: What kind of freedom was this? Was it possible to be free if you didn't have the means to care for yourself? Was it possible to be free if you didn't know how to read, write, and do figures? Was it possible to be free if white men could look at your freedom papers, tear them up, and then claim you were theirs?

"What you offering us ain't freedom," Big Sam said. "It's just slavery under another way of doing it. How we ever gon' have money enough to do anything if we paying you for our food and house? We can't do figures. How we gon' know that the figures you give us are the right ones?"

"Do you have a better idea, Sam?"

I spoke up and said I did. "You said there's a war coming."

"No doubt in my mind about that."

"Well, seems to me that the war is going to make us free anyway."

"That's if the North wins."

"I understand that. Let's do this. I think we better off staying here and working for you as slaves like we always have and you taking care of all our needs. If the war frees us, then maybe the government will give us a little money to help us get our heads above water."

"And what happens if the South wins?"

"Well, if the South wins, then that's the time you can give us our freedom."

"I was just thinking something along the same lines," Big Sam agreed. "What do you say, Master Chelsea?"

Samuel Chelsea nodded. "If that's what you want, then it's a deal. But if any of you don't want to wait to be free, you can leave right now. If you stay here, you continue to be slaves. And if you want to be free, you can't remain here, but you can go wherever you want."

"It's a deal," Big Sam said, and all the other slaves agreed.

Sylvie walked back to the quarters with me and Sister Harriet.

"What you going to do?" she wanted to know. "You staying, or you going?"

"Staying," I said without hesitating. "Sister Harriet took care of me when I didn't have nobody. It's my turn to take care of her."

"You ain't got to stay on my account," Harriet responded. "I'll be fine."

Even Sylvie heard the quaver in her voice, heard the fear of someone who had been slave to another all her life and was uncertain that she knew how to be anything else, and was perhaps too old to want to find out.

I put my arm around Harriet's shoulder and hugged her tightly. "And what if I want to stay? What if I couldn't live with myself if I left, knowing you were here by yourself?"

I pretended not to see the tears that came into Harriet's eyes. "Well, since you put it that way, I reckon it's all right."

"I suppose I'll be staying, too," Sylvie added. "If that's all right with you," she added softly.

"That's fine with me," I responded.

When Harriet and I were alone that night, she said, "I appreciate what you said today about staying on my account. And if you were really my Nat, I would insist that you stay. But you're not Nat. And your god sent you here to do something important. You not a slave like the rest of us. You just pretending until you finish up what you were sent here to do, and then your god will take you on back to Africa."

"Amma came to take me back and I refused to go."

"Why did you do that, son?"

"I'm not sure. I suppose I feel like this is where I belong now."

" 'Cause this is where she's buried?"

"That's one of the reasons, but you're another."

"Well, I want to thank you for wanting to take care of me. I don't know what I'd do if I had to be here by myself."

5

In the slave quarters, grief had deadened everyone's heart. Even though the slaves knew they had only to ask Master Chelsea and he would give them a piece of paper saying they were free, they were reluctant to take a freedom so covered with blood.

Most of them had thought Gabriel was more than a little crazy, but they missed hearing him talk about how evil white people were and what should be done to them. He had said things they were afraid to think. When they wondered what Gabriel would have said about Master Chelsea offering them their freedom, it was almost as if they could hear him: "Would he have set you free if his stringy-haired daughter hadn't been killed? If it had just been niggers who died, do you honestly believe Master Chelsea would have set you free? And what kind of freedom is he offering you? You free to go walking down the big road until some white man come along and grab you and say you the slave what ran away from him. If you don't have any money in your pocket, then you not free. Master Chelsea don't care nothin' about y'all. He just tryin' to make himself feel better 'cause his daughter got killed."

But eventually, some of the slaves did take that free-

dom Master Chelsea had offered. One was Betty, Sylvie's
mother. She said if she didn't try and be free, then George
had died for nothing. He had died 'cause he wanted her to
be free, so free was what she was going to be. Betty asked
Sylvie to come with her. Sylvie was torn. She had wanted to
be free for as long as she could remember, but freedom
was mixed up in her mind with Nat. She knew that was
silly, but that's how it was.

——

I had no second thoughts about staying. As much as I
did not want to be a slave, Harriet needed me. And for reasons I did not understand, I needed to be near Ellen. So I
gave myself over to these very human emotions of respon-
sibility and grief, thinking, hoping, that in knowing such
emotions, I would learn what the nyama of this land
needed for their rest.

Late each afternoon, I went to the plantation cemetery
and sat beside Ellen's grave. I liked it there among the
dead. It was quiet and still, and I felt a strange kind of
peace, as if here among the dead was where I belonged, but
without dying just yet.

After sitting beside Ellen's grave for a while, I would
always wander among the unmarked graves of slaves,
apologizing silently for unknowingly stepping on where
someone lay buried. Then, near dusk, I would make my
way back to the slave quarters.

One evening as I left the cemetery, I noticed a thin fog
in the air. I wondered where it was coming from because it
was too warm for fog. However, the closer I came to the

slave quarters, the fog became so thick I could scarcely find my way to the cabin.

"It's so foggy out there I could hardly see," I said to Harriet as I came in.

She frowned. "I come in a little while ago and it wasn't foggy then."

"Well, it's foggy now. Go see for yourself."

Harriet went to the door and opened it. "Son?" she called to me. "You all right?"

"I'm fine. Why?"

"Then where's that fog you talking about? I don't see a thing out here except the moon coming up and a clear sky."

I went to the door and looked. If anything, the fog was thicker now. "You don't see it?" I asked.

Harriet looked at me. "If you was anybody else, I'd say the fog was in your head. But you a Africa man. You see things us don't." She turned and went back inside.

I stood in the doorway and looked at the fog closely. It was more dense around some cabins than others. The more I examined it, the more I realized that the fog was coming from the cabins themselves. Around some it billowed out in steady clouds. Around others it seeped out beneath the doors and through cracks in the walls. I did not understand. This was neither fog nor smoke. Then what was it?

The next morning, I looked out the door as soon as I awoke. The fog was still there. I watched as slaves went to the well to draw water. They moved slowly, as if their bones were almost too heavy to lift. The sound of their voices was muffled, as if someone or something had a hand over their mouths.

As people headed toward the fields, I was startled when I saw that the fog was coming from their chests, some in heavy clouds and others in wisps. And fog was not coming from everyone.

I looked at myself. To my surprise, fog was coming from me in a steady stream. But when I went back inside the cabin and looked at Harriet, none was coming from her.

All that day, I thought about what I had seen. Something was going on, but I had no idea what. And why wasn't the fog coming from everyone? I decided to make a list of those from whom fog was coming. There was a lot around the cabin of Cleopatra, who was Henry's wife. Henry had been one of the twelve. Big Sam and Cleora's cabin was so covered by fog it was almost hidden. Dinah's was, too, and Horace had been one of the twelve. There was also a lot of fog around Sylvie's cabin, and of course George had been one of the twelve. When I finished, it was clear that the fog was only coming from those who had loved one of the twelve. Was this fog the nyama of the twelve? No, I decided, because the fog was coming from inside people.

I became concerned the next morning when I saw that the fog was thicker than it had been the day before. When Sylvie stopped by for me to walk with her to the field, the cabin became so filled with fog I could barely see her even though she was standing close enough that I could touch her. She came to me, put her arms around my back, her head on my shoulder.

"What's wrong?" I asked.

She was silent for a long while. Finally, she said, in almost a whisper, "I miss George so much."

I remembered her brother telling me, after I had killed Gabriel, that everything was my fault. If anger could have annihilated me, his would have. "What was he like?" I asked, sensing that she wanted to, needed to talk about him.

She stepped back, a sad smile on her face. "My brother was like a roaring fire. If he liked you, he liked you all the way. And if he hated you, he hated you all the way. He wasn't no halfway man. Uh-uh! I remember the time when the ol' white overseer, Master Pearson, was still here. We was picking corn and Master Pearson say George wasn't picking fast enough. George say he was picking as fast as he could pick. Master Pearson told him to stop his back talk. George say he wasn't back talking, just trying to explain he was doing his best. Master Pearson was on his horse and he had this long whip looped over the saddle horn. He took that whip and swung it at George. George, he stepped to the side, grabbed that whip, and pulled." She laughed. "That white man came off that horse, and wham! Hit the ground! George jerked the whip out of his hand, grabbed it by the handle, and drew his arm back like he was going to put a few lashes on Master Pearson. That white man held his hands and started pleading, 'Don't hit me! Please don't hit me!' That was the last day any of us had to worry about that piece of white trash. Master Chelsea was more mad at him for trying to whip one of us than he was at George for protecting himself." She laughed again. "George could get on your nerves something terrible, but I still miss him more than I ever thought I would."

She wiped at her eyes, took a deep breath, and sighed. "Well, no point in standing here talking about George. Talk ain't gon' bring him back." She gave a weak smile. "Walk me to the field?"

As she had been talking, I was surprised to see the fog around her thinning. The more she talked, the more the fog dissipated. But when she stopped, it came back. I shook my head slowly. "Not this morning. But before you go, can I ask you a question?"

"What's on your mind?"

"I haven't seen you cry over what happened to George."

She gave an awkward shrug. "Wouldn't do no good. Us slaves got so much to cry over, I be afraid that once I started crying I might not be able to stop. Why you ask me that?"

"I was just thinking. I remember one time Fulani told me that among his people, when a person died, everyone grieved. People would cry and scream, sometimes for days. He said that if a woman's husband died, she would break a dish or bowl he ate from as a sign that he wasn't coming back."

"What they do all that for?" Sylvie wanted to know. "When a person's dead, they dead."

It was my turn to shrug. "I just remembered it and thought it was interesting."

"Well, I got to get to the field, not that anybody would notice if I wasn't there. Master Chelsea don't seem like he care anymore about anything since Miss Ellen got killed, and Big Sam ain't been doing much overseeing since Little Sam got killed. Seems like ain't nothing right since everything that happened over at the Foster plantation. What's gon' become of us, Nat?"

I shook my head. She kissed me on the cheek and left. I sat down on the edge of my bed, thinking about what she had said, thinking about the fog starting to go away from around her and then coming back. I thought I was beginning to understand.

There had been no outward expressions of grief for the twelve since the morning they were killed. I doubted that it would ever be possible for any of the slaves to completely express what they felt at seeing the bodies of the children they had nursed at their breasts, the husbands they had lain with to create children, and the brothers they loved, dragged along the ground until they were little more than shredded, bloody pieces of meat. Then to have those bodies thrown into the river with less ceremony than corncobs thrown into a pig sty? I wondered if what I was seeing as fog was grief that did not know itself.

That afternoon, I met Sylvie as she was leaving the field. "You know everybody better than I do," I said. "Would you go to everybody who lost somebody in the attack on the Foster plantation and ask them what it is they miss most about the person?"

She frowned. "Why you want to know that?"

"I can't say just yet. But just get them to tell you something about the person like you just told me about George."

"Well, I don't know that I need to do all that. I know

every last one of them. Been knowing them ever since I was born. I could probably tell you what you want to know."

"That would be fine."

Instead of going to the slave quarters, I took her to the carpentry shed, where she told me stories about the life of the plantation. There was Horace, who "just loved to dance. He loved to dance so much that he didn't need no music. He said he had all the music he needed inside his head."

Little Sam knew all about the weather. He could look up in the sky at the clouds and know when it was going to rain. "You remember the big storm that come through here when we was children?"

"Which one?" I asked, not able to find any storm among Nat's memories.

"The real big one! How could you forget that storm? It was a day when the sky was just as clear and blue as it could be. Little Sam told his papa that a storm was coming. Big Sam looked at him like he was crazy. 'What storm you talking about, boy? Ain't a cloud in the sky.' Little Sam say the wind done change direction, that the wind was coming up from the south and it was going to be blowing in a big storm. Well, the corn was just about ready to be picked, but Big Sam wanted to leave it on the stalks a few days more. But he trusted Little Sam, so he set us to picking corn. Lawd, have mercy! I ain't never picked so much corn so fast in all my days. Sun went down and we was still picking. But we noticed that clouds had begun to move in. After a while, we couldn't see the stars. The wind started to blow a little harder. It was way up in the night before we got all that corn picked and put away in the corncribs in the barn. Wouldn't you know it, but toward day it started raining. Have mercy! That rain came down like bullets and the wind near 'bout blew us away from here. All the other plantations lost everything, but not us. We had plenty corn to get us and the cows through the winter."

As she talked, I could feel a weight begin lifting from her spirit. By the time she finished telling me stories that afternoon, no fog was coming from her.

"You not going to tell me why you wanted to know all that?" she asked again.

"You'll find out."

"When?"

"Soon. Hopefully by tomorrow."

———

I knew what I had to do, but I didn't think I had time to carve twelve statues. Each day the fog was getting more and more dense around everyone from whom it poured. Some of them were in danger of being suffocated by their grief. I had no choice; I had to carve twelve statues and not sleep until I had them done. The first thing was to find enough dead wood in the forest.

As I opened the door of the carpentry shed, a large red snake lay on the ground, blocking my way.

"Lebe! Have you brought me wood as you did when I carved the statues for Amina and Josiah?"

The serpent did not move.

"I have work to do," I said impatiently. "If you have not come to help me, then let me by. I don't have much time."

Lebe raised himself until his eyes were looking into

mine. Then he pushed against me, forcing me back inside.

"What are you doing?" I asked, a little afraid for the first time.

Lebe continued pressing himself against me, pushing me until I was in the back room. Then the serpent stopped, blocking the doorway.

I didn't understand what was happening. Was Amma so angry I had decided to stay in this land that he sent Lebe to kill me? I stared into the serpent's eyes but saw no malice. Instead, I saw what I thought might be a plea. But for what?

I had no idea. All I knew was that I had to get busy carving statues before it was too late. How could I, with Lebe blocking the only way out?

But one does not argue with a god. If Lebe was stopping me from going out, there was a reason.

"Do you want me to stay in here?" I asked.

The serpent nodded once.

"But why? I can't do what I need to do if I'm in here." But as the words came out of my mouth, I remembered! Quickly I went to the wooden box on the floor against the back wall. I opened it and took out one of the statues Fulani had carved. I held it up to Lebe.

"Is this what you wanted me to remember?"

The plea vanished from the serpent's eyes and he nodded once. Then Lebe shrank until he was no bigger than a small snake, wriggled through a crack in the floor, and was gone.

6

I worked through the night and finished just as the sun was suffusing the morning sky with orange colors. I went to Sylvie's cabin.

"Go tell the families of the twelve to stay away from the field this morning and come to the burying ground," I told her when she came to the door.

"You not gon' tell me what this is about?"

"You'll find out soon enough. Just tell them what I said."

"What about them that ain't lost nobody? Can they come?"

"If they want."

I was weary as I walked back to the carpentry shed and put twelve of Fulani's statues in a large burlap bag, slung it over my shoulder, and went to the cemetery. I wasn't sure if what I had in mind would work, but I had to give it a try. I knew that no nyama would go to live in these statues, because Fulani had tried that and failed. But if the statues could not bring peace to the dead, maybe they could bestow peace on the living.

At the back edge of the slaves' burying ground, I took each statue and pressed it into the ground, spacing them in a straight line, three feet apart from each other. Then I sat to the side and waited for the arrival of the others.

They came slowly, obediently, just as the sun cleared the eastern horizon. Around some the fog was thicker and heavier, and they moved as if each step caused the most excruciating pain.

I was surprised, but every slave on the plantation came. They looked curiously at the row of statues standing to the right of where I sat.

I asked them to sit. I wanted my words to be true. I waited until everyone was seated and quiet. Then I began:

"You know me as Nat, Sister Harriet's grandson, and Gabriel and Lizzie's boy. My real name is Ekundayo. I am a spirit that was brought from Africa. The one you know as Nat gave me his body to house both his spirit and mine."

People looked at each other, confused, not understanding what they had just heard. I was not surprised.

"I know this may be difficult to believe," I continued. "But it is true. I was sent here by Amma, the chief god of my people. Those you call white people and I call Soul Stealers have committed horrors against our people, both in Africa and here. They do not know that they are causing grief, not only for us but for the world. Grief that is not tended turns into anger. Anger that is not heeded congeals into hatred. Hatred putrefies into violence against oneself and others.

"I look at you and I see grief like a thick shawl hanging from many of your shoulders. But this is not a shawl that keeps you warm. This shawl is cold and heavy.

"How could it not be that way? Twelve men who lived among us are dead, their bodies treated with less respect than would have been given to a dead horse."

"That's the truth," someone said, as another started weeping quietly.

"Those bodies were thrown into the river as if they were nothing more than bones thrown to a dog in the yard."

"Oh, Lawd! Oh, Lawd!"

The crying became more general.

"We were not given the chance to say goodbye to those we loved. We were not given the chance to tend their bruised and bloodied bodies. We were not given the opportunity to hold their bloodied and broken bodies in our arms."

Someone shrieked, "Why did they do that to my baby? Why?"

"But that does not mean we cannot mourn our losses." I pointed to the first statue in the row of twelve, then looked at Sylvie, who was sitting right in front of me. "This is to mark the death of George." I pointed to letters I had carved across the statue's abdomen. "That's his name." Beneath the name was carved a tiny flame. "This flame represents George's fiery spirit."

Sylvie came forward, tears flowing down her face, and ran her hands softly up and down the length of the statue. Then, tenderly, she traced the letters G-E-O-R-G-E. She looked up at me.

"That's what his name looks like?"

I nodded. She smiled through her tears.

I pointed to the next statue. "Little Sam," I said quietly, pointing to the name. Below his name I had carved a small cloud with tiny lines representing rain falling from it. Big Sam and Cleora came forward.

I continued down the line, reading each name I had carved into a statue, and the family members came and sat before these "tombstones" over graves that did not exist. But it did not matter to them that the bodies did not lie in the ground beneath. What mattered was that those who remained now had a place to come to and let the tears flow, a place where they could talk aloud to the dead one, and speak of their love and the lacerating pain of cruel loss.

Harriet sat beside the last statue, on which was carved GABRIEL. Beneath the name I had carved a Bible. Harriet was not crying. She was too ashamed to do that.

"I done you wrong," she said softly. "I never did like you, and I ain't saying that I do now. But I was too stubborn to give you your due for making my Lizzie happy and for giving me Nat. And that wasn't right. You ain't got to like somebody to give them their due. And I was wrong to keep you away from your boy. I was afraid he would want to be with you rather than me, and then I wouldn't have anybody. That wasn't fair to him. Wasn't fair to you. I still think you was a crazy man that did more harm than good. But maybe you wouldn't have turned out that way if I'd treated you better."

There were many other such conversations and still more crying and screaming. I stood to the side and watched. I was confused. The fog around those grieving was not breaking up. I had thought it would when they began expressing their grief. However, if anything, the fog was getting thicker. Grief was still poised to swallow too many of them.

Finally, the cries and screams subsided to be replaced by sounds of sniffling. Then Dinah chuckled. She looked around until she saw me standing to the side, alone. She beckoned for me to come to her.

"I don't know what you say your name is now. To me, you still look like Nat." She looked at the others. "Don't he still look like Nat?" she asked everyone.

"Sho do" came back the responses.

"I don't know nothing about Africa," she continued. "Maybe you a spirit like you say. But then again, your papa was Gabriel, and Gabriel was always seeing things none of the rest of us did. To me, you sound just like him, only not as crazy."

There was a lot of laughter.

"So you still Nat to me, and, Nat, I just want to thank you for this." She pointed to the statue with HORACE carved on it. "And I especially want to thank you for putting that drawing on there of a man dancing." She laughed. "Me and Horace growed up here together, and ever since he was a baby he loved to dance. His mama, she dead now, she said when she was carrying him, he was dancing inside her. Sometimes I wished I could be inside his head to hear what he was hearing that got him to moving his feet the way he did."

As she continued talking about Horace, I noticed that the fog surrounding her began to thin. When she finished, the fog coalesced into a long, thin braid and entered Horace's statue.

Others were now eager to tell stories about their dead, and as they did, the fog around each one twisted itself into a braid and melted into the statue bearing the name of the one whose memory had been evoked. By the time the last person finished, sorrow had turned to joy, as everyone was laughing and crying at the same time.

Finally, people began drifting away, but no one left without shaking my hand, or giving me a hug and thanking me. As they walked back toward the plantation, they moved with an ease and lightness they had not felt in the weeks since the deaths of the twelve.

I watched them go, pleased that I got the result I wanted, though not in the way I had thought. Not only had they needed to express their grief, but, more important, it seemed, they needed to tell the stories. In the stories was the love that would endure, as long as someone remembered the stories, and told them to another.

However, as my eyes followed the slaves back to the plantation, I noticed that a thin haze still hung over the slave quarters. I didn't understand. Everyone had cried. Everyone had told their stories. The fog was supposed to be gone.

"I'm very proud of you," Sylvie said softly, interrupting my thinking.

Seeing the haze that remained over the slave quarters, I wasn't sure I had accomplished anything.

"But I'm not sure what I should call you. Nat? Ekundayo? I mean, who are you?"

"I guess I'm both."

"Are you more one than the other?"

I thought for a moment. "Sometimes. When I am building something from wood, I am more Nat. Most of the time, though, I'm Ekundayo."

"Is that what you want me to call you?"

I hesitated. "Yes. It would be nice to hear that name on someone's lips. Especially yours."

"Can I ask you a question?" Sylvie took my hand and walked toward the end of the cemetery where the whites were buried. She stopped in front of the mound of dirt over Ellen's grave. "When I was listening to everybody telling stories about who they loved, I thought about her." She nodded at the mound of dirt. "Nat? What was she like?"

I smiled and sat down. "She was my friend," I said softly. "We grew up together. We always seemed to know what the other was feeling. There was this one time. We couldn't have been more than five years old. Grandmama had sent me down to the barn for something. Ellen was in the kitchen with her. Suddenly, Ellen shouted, 'Nat fell,' and hurried out the door. And sure enough, I had tripped and fallen just as I got to the barn and hit my head on the door. I don't know how she knew, but she did." I continued talking about Ellen, telling Sylvie about her smile and the sparkle in her eyes and her laugh, which sounded like water flowing over rocks. When I finished, there were tears in my eyes.

We sat silently at the grave for a long while. Finally, when we stood up, I saw that the last sheet of thin fog had disappeared from over the slave quarters.

The next morning was almost like a normal one on the plantation, with the slamming of doors, laughter, and loud talking as people made ready to go to the fields. After walking Sylvie out to where she would work that day, I went to the carpentry shed. When I walked in, Ellen was sitting in the chair at the far corner of the room.

Nathaniel.

I smiled, my love for her filling my body with quiet joy.

Ellen.

What you did yesterday was wonderful. It helped them so much.

Yes. Everyone seems almost back to their normal selves this morning.

No. I mean, the twelve.

You mean, Gabriel and the others?

Yes. They had been so afraid no one would want to remember them, that no one cared. They were a little surprised it was you.

I had not done it for them, at least not intentionally. *I don't understand. You know them? You see them?*

Not as much as my husband and his parents see them.

I shook my head. *Forgive me for repeating myself, but I don't understand.*

It's actually quite simple and, I daresay, almost poetic. My in-laws and my husband were some of the meanest slave owners in the state of Virginia. So the twelve and my husband and his parents have to live together and work things out. I don't know how it is for Gabriel and the other eleven, but I can tell you: for Gregory and his parents, they are in hell!

She laughed her wonderful high laugh. *But Gabriel has to make peace with Sally, the Foster plantation cook, and she is not in a peace-making mood. And Ezekiel has to make peace with me, his daughter, and his granddaughter. They're quite upset with him for killing me. And I am, too.*

I miss you, Ellen.

I can't say I'm sorry you do. As long as you miss me, I know you won't have forgotten me.

How could I ever forget you?

Oh, time changes things, you know. There is going to be a war, and when it's over, you're going to marry Sylvie. The two of you will move out to Nebraska and have three children. You won't have time to think about me, and after a while your memories of me will fade. The worst part about being dead is the fear of being forgotten, that after a generation or two, no one will even remember that you lived. When that happens, well, that's when you're really dead.

I will never forget you.

But when you die, your children will remember you; they won't remember me. When you die, I will die. I don't want us to die, Nathaniel. Not ever.

That won't happen.

I hope not. I love you, Nathaniel. I always will.

And I love you, Ellen.

Tell Sylvie I forgive her, and she doesn't have to come visit my grave every day.

I beg your pardon?

You didn't know. Every day she comes to my grave to tell me how sorry she is about what she did. She's cried a lot about that. She's probably done more crying about that than her brother. To those of us who are dead, the tears of the living are the same as water to you. She's a good woman. You'll be happy with her. Not as happy as you would have been with me. She laughed. *But there was no place for us in the world the way it is now. Maybe we'll come back later and be to each other everything we couldn't be now. Oh. One other thing. If you want her to call you Nathaniel, it's all right with me.*

And she was gone.

7

Samuel Chelsea sat in his office, a glass of rum in his hand, a half-full bottle on the desk, staring at the papers strewn across its surface. He did not know what he had hoped to accomplish by offering his slaves their freedom. He had thought it would make him feel better to do something that would have made Ellen proud of him. But the freedom he had offered had been so worthless, practically all of the slaves had turned it down. What could be said about a man who couldn't give away freedom?

Well, there was plenty to be said, it seemed, to a man whose slaves carried out an uprising. He picked up one of the letters on his desk and didn't have to read more than the first paragraph to know it was spewing outrage at him for having "a plantation of bloodthirsty niggers who killed God-fearin' white people." He had to laugh. Greg Foster and that son of his, God-fearing? They were so mean that if anybody was going to be afraid, it was probably God. Shakespeare had it wrong: the good was not interred with people's bones and neither did the evil live after them. What happened was that a whole host of lies rose up, and newspaper editorial writers called a mean son-of-a-bitch like Greg Foster a kindly old man who didn't deserve to die at the hands of niggers.

But truth did not matter. Greg was a saint now, while he was a nigger-loving devil. When he walked along the street in town, people turned their backs when they saw him coming. Just the other day, someone had spit a stream of tobacco juice on his shoes. Things weren't any better in Richmond. Lawyers and businessmen he thought were friends were too busy when he dropped by their offices. He had half a mind to say the hell with it and go up North where nobody knew who he was. He knew that Gabriel's Attack, as the newspapers called it, had been covered in the Northern papers and his name was mentioned in all the articles, but no one up there knew what he looked like. What was to keep him from changing his name and going to some place like Philadelphia or Boston and practicing law? He had a fair amount of money in the bank, though he'd told the slaves he didn't have any. He felt bad about lying to them, but then again, he didn't. He had to think about himself, and he had enough money to find a decent place and to live off of for a year or so before he would need to find a favorable situation. And who knew? He might find a rich widow in need of companionship.

But that left the plantation. Nobody would buy it, not with talk of war in the air. And he doubted that he could sell any of the slaves, not when it became known that they were "Chelsea plantation niggers."

Feeling the presence of someone, he looked up to see Nat standing in the door. He put down the glass of rum, ashamed for Nat to see him drinking.

—

I had been standing for a while in the parlor outside Master Chelsea's office looking at him. He was sitting at his desk, his head bowed like he was praying, but I didn't think he was. I had never seen anything God-fearing about Master Chelsea.

He didn't look any better than he had the morning he came to confess to me and Sister Harriet. If anything, he looked worse because he had stopped shaving and his face was covered with a white beard. There was a glass of liquor and a bottle on the desk. He emptied the glass like it was filled with water and refilled it and drank some more.

He started to raise his head and I stepped quickly to the side, out of his line of sight but where I could still see him. There was fear in his eyes, as if he had been put in a cage and couldn't find the door to get out. I had not thought about it until that moment, but it seemed like slave owners were caught in the same cage as their slaves. But that did not make me feel sorry for Master Chelsea or any of the others. Unlike us, they had walked into that cage with nobody's help.

Now Master Chelsea wanted out and he didn't know the way. If he sold away the woman he loved and his own child, if he was so full of jealousy that he would marry his daughter off to a man she didn't love, I had no doubt that if he could sell us and leave here, he wouldn't hesitate to do it, despite all the nice words he'd said to us the other day about giving us our freedom.

The longer I stood there looking at him, the more I wanted to put my hands around his white neck and choke him. But that wouldn't have accomplished anything, and I had important work to do. Master Chelsea didn't matter enough for me to kill him.

As he reached for the bottle of liquor to refill the glass he had just emptied, I came and stood in the doorway.

He looked up, startled. He put down the bottle and shoved it and the glass to the edge of the desk.

"What can I do for you, Nat?"

"I was wondering if you had some paper, a pen, and ink that I could borrow?"

Samuel Chelsea narrowed his eyes. "You tellin' me you can read and write?"

I wondered if I had made a mistake. Should I have waited until after he went to bed that night, then come in the house and taken what I needed? Maybe, but if I got caught, he could call me a thief, and I'm not a thief.

"Ellen taught me," I said simply.

"Did she teach you to do numbers, too?" he asked, not surprised that Ellen had taught me to read and write.

"Yes, sir."

Samuel nodded. "How much paper you want?"

"As much as I can get."

"Mind if I ask what you're going to write?"

"I want to write down everything I remember about Ellen, so if there ever comes a time when my mind forgets, the paper will remember."

Samuel Chelsea looked at me quizzically, as if he didn't understand. But I imagine when he thought about his life, all he saw were things he wanted to forget. He stared at me for a moment, but this time as if he was thinking about something. Then he pointed to a bookcase to his right.

"Down there are books with nothing but blank pages in them. I got them years ago to put my thoughts on various matters in." He laughed sadly. "Never put pen to paper. Guess I didn't have any thoughts worth putting down." He reached down and pulled out one of the blank books and handed it to me. He pointed to the inkwell on his desk and the quill pen next to it. "You can take them out in the parlor if you want and do your writing there. Probably a little more comfortable than doing it in the kitchen."

"Thank you, sir. I appreciate it."

Just as I started to leave, Master Chelsea said, "Nat?"

I turned around. "Sir?"

Master Chelsea handed me one of the pieces of paper from his desk. "Read that out loud."

I took the sheet of paper. It was a legal document with some words I had never seen, but without difficulty I read it aloud.

Samuel Chelsea smiled. "You can read as well as I can. How would you like to run the plantation for me?"

"I beg your pardon?"

"Just for a little while. I need to get away. Too many sad memories here for me. And with the war coming, I can't sell this place, and I wouldn't sell any of you all. I need you to keep an eye on things while I'm gone. Big Sam is a good overseer. Harriet takes care of the house. I need somebody who can take care of the mail. Read it, make a decision, and, if it's very important, get word to me. You can do that, can't you?"

I looked Samuel Chelsea in the eye. "I'm sure I can," I said firmly.

Samuel laughed nervously. "I know you can, too. Then it's a deal." He extended his hand and we shook. "Now that that's taken care of, I can start making my arrangements to go away. Tomorrow, I'll sit down with you and go over all the things you'll need to know. It's nothing very complicated. Just a lot of details that can give a man a serious headache if he isn't careful."

I once again started to walk out. "Here, Nat. Why don't you sit here at my desk? It's going to be yours from now on, so you might as well get used to it. I have some things to do upstairs. Sit here and do your writing."

I wrote through the morning and into the afternoon, remembering as much as I could about Ellen. There were moments of tears, but these were tears of gratitude that she had been part of my life and I of hers. I didn't know if anyone would ever read what I wrote. Maybe it would become a book someday and people in the far-off future would read Ellen's story and feel like they had known her also.

—

That evening, I went to Big Sam's cabin and told him about my talk with Master Chelsea. "Ain't nothing for him here now that Miss Ellen is dead. He wants to leave everything in your and my hands."

Big Sam laughed dryly. "The white folks won't talk to him no more. That's the real reason he leaving us to sink or swim on our own. Let him go. I think we can make it. The plantation is just about self-sufficient. We need to train up somebody to be a blacksmith, now that Ezekiel ain't with us. But when it comes to food and the like, everything we need, we raise. You can build anything what need building. Master Chelsea just got in a new shipment of cloth to make new garments out of, so we don't need to be concerned about that.

"The only problem I see is the other white folks. If they had their way, they'd come over here and kill all of us to make us pay for the twelve. If they get wind that he's left, then we might be in trouble."

"Well, we can cross that bridge if it comes to us."

Big Sam laughed. "What are your plans for the plantation?"

"To teach everybody to read."

"When you gon' start?" Cleora asked.

"Soon as Master Chelsea's carriage is out of sight 'round the curve toward town." They laughed.

The next morning, when I went to the house and sat down at the desk in the study to read what I had written the day before, Ellen was sitting in the chair on the other side.

Nathaniel. What you wrote is so beautiful. Thank you. I can't stay long today, but I wanted you to know: my father is not coming back. When the war breaks out, he will think he can buy his way back into good favor with all of his Virginia friends by becoming a spy for the South. He's going to be caught and executed. Don't worry about the war. Soon after the war starts, some Northern soldiers will come through here and tell everybody that they are free. A lot of the young men on the plantation will leave. The rest of you will be safe here, however. I'll take care of that. And don't worry about getting whatever you need. I'll take care of that, too. And if you ever need me, just say my name. You'll know where I am."

And she wove herself into a long braid, hovered over the

pages I had written about her, then disappeared into them.

I smiled, then closed the book. Just as I started to get up, someone sat down in the chair where Ellen had just sat.

He was an old black man, but I didn't know who he was. He sat as if waiting for me to do something. But I had no idea what he wanted. He pointed toward the bottom shelf of the bookcase where the blank books were. I took one from the shelf. The old man motioned for me to pick up the pen. I did so. Annoyed that I still didn't know what he wanted, the old man motioned for me to open the blank book. When I did, he began talking.

My name is Mose. I was born right here on this planta-
tion in seventeen hundred and eighty-seven. My mother's
name was Bertha and my father's name was James.

And I began to write. Mose told me the joys and the sorrows of his life. He had more joys than sorrows because he refused to see his sorrows as sorrows. When his story came to an end, his nyama plaited itself into a braid and disappeared into the pages of the book where I had written his story.

That was when I finally realized: I had found the answer! I knew how to care for the nyama. In a land where there were so many, no one could ever make enough statues for them. Here, nyama would find their resting places in stories, stories I would write down, and if there came a time when no one was left to remember, the dead would not be forgotten. The stories I wrote down would remember.

Already someone else was sitting in the chair Mose had just occupied. I turned the page, dipped the quill in the inkwell, and as the nyama started to speak, I began writing.

EPiLOGUE

Nathaniel and Sylvie Ekundayo, my great-grandparents, left Virginia after the war. Sister Harriet had died in her sleep early one morning a few weeks near the war's end. My great-grandfather put her in the ground, then carved a statue and hid it in a dark corner, high on a shelf in the kitchen pantry. He knew her nyama needed to be near the kitchen and not in a book. Next to the statue he also put the brooch Ellen had given him.

Before setting out for Nebraska, he took Sylvie to a little island off the coast of South Carolina where he found a white man and a black woman and their two small children. Josiah and Amina thought there was something familiar about the man. There was an intensity in his eyes they had seen in only one other person, but he was buried in their meadow. Or was he?

My great-grandparents didn't know exactly where Nebraska was, but when they came to a place where the land and the sky were so long and wide that they touched at a horizon so far away they could scarcely see it, Nathaniel stopped. It looked like where his people lived in Africa. They built a sod house on the plains and had three children, two boys, named Nathaniel and George, and a girl named Ellen.

My great-grandfather Nathaniel lived to be an old man and died a year after Sylvie died in a flu epidemic, but he didn't die in the way we normally think of death. His daughter, Ellen, lived with him, she being the only one of her siblings to whom the nyama would tell their stories. The stories nyama have told members of my family through the generations are kept in books, now in my possession, called *Time's Memory*.

Though technically not the story of an nyama, my grandmother, Ellen, rightly chose to put her description of Nathaniel's "death" as the last entry in her father's volume of *Time's Memory*:

"If I had not seen it, I do not know if I would have believed it. However, having seen it, I must believe it. I am the daughter of Nathaniel Ekundayo. What might be strange for others is normal for me.

"This morning my father was up at dawn as usual. He made a cup of tea and went outside. It was a chilly morning. The first snow has not come yet, but one could feel its advent in the wind. I was upstairs and I saw him walk out and look at the rising sun. As he stood there, sipping at his tea, he seemed to be waiting for something. But no one ever comes here, and there is not another house in any direction for twenty miles.

"Suddenly, I saw his face brighten as if he saw the person he was expecting. But it wasn't a who. There, as if it had crawled out of the rising sun, was a serpent of a deep red color. It was as long as the space between now and the tomorrow which never comes, and as big around as the past which always is.

"I had heard my father speak many times about Lebe, but I never thought I would see him. Yet there he was, and I knew he had come for my father. I wanted to run down the stairs and outside and pull my father back into the house. But I didn't.

"I'd had a suspicion that my father's time to live in the world of the ancestors was near. Almost a month ago, he said that the nyama had stopped coming to tell him their stories. We both knew it was time for him to prepare to join them.

"I watched Lebe weave gracefully across the flat earth until he was at my father's feet. Father leaned over and stroked Lebe on the head as if he were a cat. Lebe's tongue flicked in and out. Though my father's lips did not move, I knew he and Lebe were conversing. At one point, my father's head went back and I heard his wonderful, loud laugh. I suppose if one has to have a last memory of her father, then his laugh is a good one to have.

"Finally, Lebe lifted part of his long body from the ground and slowly began winding himself around Nathaniel Ekundayo. Father disappeared within the blood-red coils. Around and around the serpent went. Finally, he stopped, stretched his body, and once more lay flat on the earth. My father was nowhere to be seen. Lebe moved sinuously back in the direction of the sun, where he disappeared.

"I sat down immediately and wrote this account because I knew it was what my father would have wanted.

Now I wait eagerly for my father to come so I can record his story."

However, to my grandmother's great disappointment, her father's nyama did not tell her his story. She recorded the stories of many nyama, but not the one she wanted to record most of all. My mother, Ellen, recorded the stories of many nyama, but it turned out that the telling of Nathaniel's was to be my task.

By the time I was born, all memories of Nathaniel Ekundayo had vanished from my family. All that remained was the family tradition that in each generation, the first son had to be named Nathaniel, and the first daughter Ellen, and that the nyama would choose one child of each generation to record their stories. No one knew why. So I was named Nathaniel. I was to be my parents' only child.

I was eight when one night, as my mother was tucking me in bed, she sat down on the edge of the bed and asked me if I ever heard voices, or felt as if I wanted to write stories about people I had never known and never heard of. I didn't know what she was talking about. That was when she explained the family tradition of recording the stories of spirits of the dead. That was the word she used—spirits, not nyama. While I did not forget her words, I did not think about them either. Then, one day during my junior year of high school, I was sitting in math class, not my favorite one by any means, and was looking out the window not thinking about much of anything. Suddenly, an old black woman appeared. She wasn't outside, nor was she in the classroom. The only way I can explain it is to say she was in the window glass itself, except her voice, sounding as ancient as wind, was speaking inside me. For a moment I thought I was going crazy, then I remembered my mother's words about the spirits and how they had chosen our family to record their stories. Quickly, I opened my notebook and began writing what she was saying.

When I went home, I waited anxiously for my mother, even though I knew it would be at least an hour, maybe two, before she left the office. But she came home early that day and I told her. That was when she took me to a closet in her and my father's bedroom. There she showed me the leather-bound volumes in which she and my ancestors had recorded the stories of the spirits who had spoken to them. Then, solemnly, she took one from the bottom of the shelf and handed it to me. I opened it. The pages were blank. I understood. It was here I was to record the stories the spirits entrusted me with.

After that initial time in math class, the spirits were respectful of my time and came only when I was alone. I was grateful to them for being so considerate, as I did not know how I would explain to anyone that spirits of dead black people told me their stories.

Then, the first day of my freshman year of college, I met Ellen. The immediacy of our connection was so overwhelming, it was as if we were resuming a relationship that had been interrupted at some distant time in history. Within a week of meeting her, we both knew we had met the person with whom we'd spend eternity, and I told her about the nyama, as I now called them, having learned the name from reading the volumes of *Time's Memory* recorded by my grandmother, Nathaniel's daughter. My

Ellen understood that the dead need the living to know their stories.

We were married shortly after graduation. As part of our honeymoon, she suggested we take a trip to the Chelsea plantation. A historical society had taken it over many years before, restored it, and it was now open to the public. I had no interest in going. I didn't see what I would gain by going to the place where my great-grandparents had been slaves. Neither did it make sense why Ellen would want to go. She was from Oregon, not Virginia. But what man would be so obtuse as to refuse his bride's request on their honeymoon?

When we arrived, both of us felt something strangely familiar about the place. As we walked up the steps of the main house to the gift shop, where we could buy tickets for the tour, I stopped and turned around.

"The slave quarters were over there," I said, pointing to my left, where tall pine trees grew.

"I think you're right," she agreed.

We looked at each other and laughed nervously. A few moments later, we saw a diagram of the plantation, and the slave quarters had indeed been located where we had indicated. How could we have known that?

The tour began and, once again, I felt like I had been there before. When we came to the dining room, I wanted to stand in the corner opposite a closed door. When we entered Samuel Chelsea's study, I thought I could see myself sitting behind his desk. I wondered if I was being visited by Chelsea's nyama.

Then, as the tour guide began leading us upstairs,

something urged me to explore the house on my own. I told the tour guide I wasn't feeling well and urged Ellen to complete the tour and that I would meet her either at the car or in the gift shop.

As soon as the group was up the stairs, I opened the closed door off the dining room. I was almost certain that the long passageway I had just entered led to the plantation kitchen. And it did.

I stood in the center of the kitchen. I was looking for something, but what? And where? I didn't have much time before the tour made its way there. Where would someone have hidden something? I mused. That was when I saw another door, to the left and behind the wood-burning cookstove.

I walked into what had been a pantry. On the shelves were both antique and facsimile kitchen utensils as well as preserving jars and tins in which rice, flour, and dried corn and beans would have been stored.

I went to the very end of the pantry and reached up in the corner of the highest shelf, as if I knew something was there. My fingers brushed two objects, one made of wood and another that felt like it might be a brooch.

I brought them out where I could see them and saw that I was holding a small statue and a cameo brooch. "I'm amazed they are still here," I whispered, but though the voice was mine, the words were not. Yet they had come from me. What was happening?

I put the statue back where I found it, though I didn't know why, but dropped the brooch in my pants pocket. I heard the tour guide and the group coming down the stairs. I saw a door leading directly from the kitchen to the outside, and I exited quickly.

I felt more than a little guilty for not telling the plantation curator what I had found. But I couldn't.

The plantation gift shop sold basket lunches—cheese, English tea crackers, pâté, and half bottles of white wine from a local winery. While Ellen got a blanket from the car, I bought two of the lunches.

"The plantation cemetery is over this way," I said to Ellen, pointing toward a line of tall pine trees.

"It's amazing how tall those trees have gotten," Ellen remarked.

We looked at each other strangely.

When we reached the cemetery, we spread the blanket on the closely mowed grass near the wrought-iron fence surrounding the Chelsea and Ramsey family graves. Samuel, Charlotte, and Ellen Chelsea's gravestones were upright, the names still plain to see.

"That's where the slaves are buried," I said, pointing to the area behind the fence which was overgrown with weeds, grasses, and wildflowers.

Ellen and I had finished eating and were enjoying the last of the wine when I took the brooch from my pocket and told her where I had gotten it. She chastised me for taking something of incalculable historical value. But then she opened it.

We both gasped when we looked at the face of the young woman on the photograph within. It could be only one person—Ellen Chelsea! But that was not what was so remarkable. The face on the photograph in the brooch was also the face of my Ellen. Because it had not been opened in more than a hundred years, the photograph had not been exposed to light or mold and was thus perfectly preserved. There was no mistaking. Ellen Chelsea and my wife were identical in every respect—the same eyes, thin lips, the shape of the brows, the same long, dark hair.

Then I became aware of a presence and looked up to see a man standing at the foot of Ellen Chelsea's grave.

"Look," I whispered to Ellen. I didn't know if she would see what I saw, but I hoped so. I needed confirmation that I was not imagining this.

"Oh, my God!" she exclaimed.

There stood a tall, thin man with skin as black as space. His face was long, his eyes were big, almost mournful. The lips were full; the hair short. In brief, I was looking at myself! I had no doubt that the figure was my ancestor, my namesake, Nathaniel Ekundayo. He looked at me, smiled, and was gone. It was then that I understood.

Although my parents are medium-brown-skinned, I am as black-skinned as one can be. I was born Nathaniel Saunders, which is my father's surname. But in college I started using Ekundayo, my great-grandfather's name, as my surname. And that is the name on my marriage certificate.

That evening, I sat on a bed in a motel room and began typing on my laptop computer. Sitting at the desk in that same motel room, Ellen began typing on her laptop. Time took each of us into her memory, where we learned that we were continuing a love story that had been interrupted. Amma was so grateful that I had found the way to bring peace to the nyama, he returned my and Ellen's nyama and forms to life so we could live the love we could not live then.

Ekundayo had not told his story to his daughter, or her daughter, because it was a story that Ellen and I had to return and tell for ourselves.

There is another reason Ellen and I were returned. We are unable to have children. If my story—our story—is not recorded now, it never will be. Our family lines are finished. Both of us worry about who will listen to the dead, record their stories, and give them the peace that comes when they have told their stories and had them written down.

It is of great concern to us because nyama multiply daily from wars, famines, disease, accidents, old age. They outnumber the living, and they roam the world, unknown, uncared for, unloved. Only recently have I understood that nyama along the coast of West Africa acquired the power to govern the winds and rains, and they send hurricanes across the oceans and into the Northern Hemisphere, exacting their revenge for what the Soul Stealers did. The spirits of the aboriginal people of the Northern Hemisphere are warming the air and the seas and melting the icecaps.

There is nothing more I can do. Ellen and I have returned to the land from which I came more than a hundred years ago as a seed in the womb of a woman named Amina. My work is done. Having spent so much of both my lives with the spirits of the dead, my remaining years will be with the living, something I am looking forward to, now that this, the last volume of *Time's Memory*, is done.

I have done all that I could. If there is to be hope for the living, someone else must care for the spirits of the dead.

Someone else.

Nathaniel Ekundayo & Ellen Chelsea
West Africa

AUTHOR'S NOTE

Novels are strange beings. It may seem odd to describe a book as a "being." But novels have lives of their own, independent of us, their authors. Sometimes, our task is to understand what it is the novel wants to be and help it become that.

Although I could not have known it then, this novel began in late May 1975. I had a major dream, one that transformed my life. In that dream there was a religious structure unlike any I had ever seen. Some five to ten years later, I happened to be looking through a book about Africa, and there was the building I had seen in my dream. It was from the Dogon people of Mali. I had such a sense of identification with that building that I "knew": this was where my African ancestors, or at least one of them, had come from. Of course, there is no way to document this, but I trusted my immediate response on seeing the photograph of that building. In the almost thirty years since that dream, I have not dreamed of Africa, nor have there been any African allusions in my dreams.

I began studying Dogon religion, but it was far more abstract and complex than I had patience for at the time. The years passed. From time to time I would buy a book of

African art, and always I would turn to the section devoted to the Dogon.

In the fall of 2003, I found myself turning again to study Dogon religion. I did not understand why I was doing so. I had had no dreams compelling me in that direction. My study of Dogon religion was particularly puzzling because the book I was about to begin work on was based on the African American legend of Stagolee. I had recorded the song "Stagolee" in 1966 on my first album of folk and original songs on the Vanguard label. A few years later, I turned that version into a folktale for my *Black Folktales*. I had been looking forward to taking Stagolee from slavery in a romp through American history. But when I sat down to write, the words, the ideas, the images simply would not come. And I was continuing to study Dogon religion.

I do a lot of "writing" sitting in the bathtub at night. That is where I work out problems I am having in a manuscript, outline what I am going to write the next day, and, sometimes, even get ideas. On one such night, an image came to me of a spirit inside an African woman on a slave ship coming to America. The spirit was conscious and aware of itself. Thus, this novel came into being.

The African religious references and names throughout are taken from Dogon religion—nyama, hogon, toguna, Lebe, Amma, et cetera.

The story is perhaps one of the most autobiographical I've ever written. Throughout my life as a writer I have felt that the spirits of dead slaves were lined up inside me, waiting patiently for me to tell their stories, and I have tried my best to do so. Perhaps I needed to write this novel as a way of understanding myself and why so much of my career has been focused on the past, on the dead.

The joy and challenge of writing novels comes when characters appear whom you had not thought of. In this novel, that was Ellen Chelsea. Her sudden appearance in the carpentry shed completely changed the trajectory and focus of this novel. I had planned to write an alternative history, in which Ekundayo and the nyama played a decisive role in the Civil War at Gettysburg and, eventually, in emancipation. But Ellen walked through a door and said, "Nathaniel." Not only did something open in Ekundayo, something opened in me.

I was thrown back to my childhood and youth growing up in the segregated South of the 1950s. I entered college in 1956, going to Fisk University in my hometown of Nashville, Tennessee. Fisk had an exchange program with a number of small white liberal arts colleges like Oberlin, Pomona, Claremont. Fisk sent students to those schools for a semester and they sent students to Fisk. Especially important during my college years were my relationships with the white female exchange students. Through friendships with them, I was introduced to experiences and points of view which had been denied to me in the segregated South. These relationships were not sexual or even romantic. There was certainly an element of innocent eroticism in the excitement we felt at quietly, and not without fear, daring to challenge a history which had forbidden and outlawed interracial relationships, laws that were still on the books in many states at the time.

And so this novel became, in a way, a tribute to all those who, in the context of their personal lives, act in ways history does not condone and, by doing so, begin to change that history.

This novel is dedicated to the memory of Anne Romaine, a young white woman from North Carolina whom I met in Nashville, Tennessee, in 1966. Anne was one of a small group of young Southern white people who dared to change their lives by joining the Civil Rights Movement and, in the process, helped change history.

Julius Lester
Belchertown, Massachusetts
25 August 2004

GLOSSARY

Amina (Ah-MEE-nah)
Woman chosen to carry the seed that becomes Ekun-dayo.

Amma (AH-MAH)
The creator god and master of life and death.

Ekundayo (A-coon-DAY-oh)
A spirit formed from the union of Lebe and the nyama of the hogon.

hogon (HOE-GON)
The religious chief and leader of the Dogon people of Mali.

Lebe (LAY-BAY)
The first hogon and the incarnation of the earth.

Menyu (MEN-you)
Amina's husband.

Nommo (NOH-moe)
Son of Amma. He is the master of speech.

nyama (En-YAH-mah)
The life force, the soul. When a person or animal dies, the nyama leaves the body.

toguna (Toe-GU-nah)
The men's meeting house where Dogon meet to make important decisions.

BOOKS CONSULTED

Beckwith, Carol, and Angela Fisher. *African Ceremonies*, Vol. 2. New York: Harry N. Abrams, 1999.

Calame-Griaule, Geneviève. *Words and the Dogon World*. Philadelphia: Institute for the Study of Human Issues, 1986.

Guggenheim, Hans. *Dogon World: A Catalogue of Art and Myth for You to Complete*. The Wunderman Foundation.

Imperato, Pascal James. *Dogon Cliff Dwellers: The Art of Mali's Mountain People*. L. Kahan Gallery Inc. / African Arts, 1986.

Spini, Tito, and Sandro Spini. *Togu Na: The African Dogon "House of Men, House of Words."* New York: Rizzoli International Publications, 1977.

van Beek, Walter E. A. (text), and Stephanie Hollyman (photographs). *Dogon: Africa's People of the Cliffs*. New York: Harry N. Abrams, 2001.

COCHRAN PUBLIC LIBRARY
174 BURKE STREET
STOCKBRIDGE, GA 30281